C000065244

Emily Harvale lives in E
although she would pref
Alps...or Canada...or any where that has several
months of snow. Emily loves snow almost as much
as she loves Christmas.

Having worked in the City (London) for several
years, Emily returned to her home town of
Hastings where she spends her days writing. And
wondering if it will snow.

You can contact her via her website, Twitter,
Facebook or Instagram.

There is also a Facebook group where fans can
chat with Emily about her books, her writing day
and life in general. Details are on the 'For You'
page of Emily's website.

Author contacts:
www.emilyharvale.com
www.twitter.com/emilyharvale
www.facebook.com/emilyharvalewriter
www.instagram.com/emilyharvale

...

Scan the code above to see all Emily's books on Amazon

Also by this author:

Highland Fling
Lizzie Marshall's Wedding
The Golf Widows' Club
Sailing Solo
Carole Singer's Christmas
Christmas Wishes – Two short stories
A Slippery Slope
The Perfect Christmas Plan – A novella
Be Mine – A novella
...

The Goldebury Bay series:

Book One – Ninety Days of Summer
Book Two – Ninety Steps to Summerhill
Book Three – Ninety Days to Christmas
...

The Hideaway Down series:

Book One – A Christmas Hideaway
Book Two – Catch A Falling Star
Book Three – Walking on Sunshine
Book Four – Dancing in the Rain
...

Hall's Cross series

Deck the Halls
The Starlight Ball
...

Michaelmas Bay series

Christmas Secrets in Snowflake Cove
Blame it on the Moonlight
...

Lily Pond Lane series

The Cottage on Lily Pond Lane – Book One
The Cottage on Lily Pond Lane – Book Two
Christmas on Lily Pond Lane

Bells and Bows

on

Mistletoe Row

Emily Harvale

ISBN 978-1-909917-38-5

Published by Crescent Gate Publishing

Print edition published worldwide 2018
E-edition published worldwide 2018

Editor Christina Harkness

Cover design by JR, Luke Brabants and Emily Harvale

For Richard.
Taken far too soon.
Your light, love and laughter will be with me,
always.

Acknowledgements

My grateful thanks go to the following:

Christina Harkness for her patience and care in editing this book.

My webmaster, David Cleworth who does so much more than website stuff.

My cover design team, JR.

Luke Brabants. Luke is a talented artist and can be found at: www.lukebrabants.com

My wonderful friends for their friendship and love. You know I love you all.

All the fabulous members of my Readers' Club. You help and support me in so many ways and I am truly grateful for your ongoing friendship. I wouldn't be where I am today without you.

My Twitter and Facebook friends, and fans of my Facebook author page. It's great to chat with you. You help to keep me (relatively) sane!

Thank you for buying this book.

Bells and Bows

on

Mistletoe Row

Chapter One

Juliet Bell slowed to a halt as she neared the narrow, humpback bridge leading to Mistletoe Row, the street where she grew up, and the salmon-pink-painted cottage that her parents and her younger sister, Zoe had called home for the last twenty years. Not that she could see the bridge at that precise moment. It had been snowing on and off since she left Bristol, but as her car crawled through the brightly lit streets of the bustling town of Mistletythe, now merely a glimmer in her rear-view mirror, it had turned heavier, culminating in a sudden white-out as she reached the bridge.

Why couldn't the blizzard have held off for ten more minutes? Five, even? Juliet was so close to home she could virtually smell the spices in her mum's mulled wine. She had hoped to be sitting beside a crackling log fire long ago, but the weather, together with an abundance of road works, had delayed her two-hundred-mile journey by at least two hours and when she glanced at her dashboard, the clock read ten-to-five. Thank goodness she didn't have far to go.

But first she had to cross the stone bridge which arched over the low-lying Mistletythe River, itself no doubt covered with a layer of ice beneath a blanket of white, and as things stood, she couldn't see either the bridge or the river. The wipers of her elderly Ford Fiesta juddered across the windscreen as they battled against the weight of snow and the fact that it was dark didn't help. She pulled on the handbrake and gave herself a moment to think.

She knew this road so well. Surely she could get across the bridge with her eyes closed? And visibility might be slightly better on the other side. Mistletoe Row only had three lampposts but at least it benefitted from the additional light given out by The Mistletoe pub, nestled on the bank of the river, the church next to that with its stained-glass windows, Dobbie's Convenience Store beside that, and the houses huddled together along the stretch of narrow road.

Her family lived at number 29 – a two-storey cottage, together with an attic room, parts of which dated back to the sixteenth century and came complete with an inglenook fireplace, restored bread oven and more blackened timber beams than you could shake a stick at. Parts of it, like the white-framed Georgian windows, were a later addition, but added long before the cottage was listed.

She could picture it as she stared out into the swirling snow. The double front doors, painted a darker shade of pink to match the façade would have a garland of holly and mistletoe atop the lintel, tied each end with large red bows. Fairy lights would be hanging from the roof soffits and warm, welcoming light would flood from the windows onto the narrow, snow-covered pavement. Inside, her mum and Zoe would be in the kitchen, the aged Aga burning at full pelt and the family dog, Cinnamon stretched out in front of it, snoring and blithely ignoring the fact that she would be in everyone's way and they would have to constantly step over her.

Juliet's dad would, no doubt, be ensconced in his library, still, after all these years, writing the history of the Bell family and their centuries living at The Grange, despite the fact that he was the Bell who lost it; a bitter pill for him to swallow even after all this time. And one Juliet didn't want to think about. Certainly not today. Besides, she had more recent worries weighing her down and as she watched the wipers judder to a halt, finally giving up their fight against the onslaught, she knew exactly how they felt.

The drive from Bristol had been hellish and she was tired and hungry, having decided not to stop for lunch along the way. But that wasn't the only reason she was feeling wretched. She hadn't told her family her news. Such tidings were always better given face-to-face. At least she hoped they were. Although telling them that she had been made redundant from her job as executive assistant to the CEO of one of the largest department store chains in the country, one week before Christmas probably wouldn't go down well, face-to-face or not. Not that she was the only one. Godfrey, Able, Jones & Company was in crisis and many stores nationwide would close their doors for the final time on Christmas Eve. The CEO was retiring; the business was restructuring. Which was another way of saying it was being sold off, bit by bit.

As if that wasn't depressing enough, at the age of thirty-six, Juliet was going to have to ask to move back home. At least until she found another job. The apartment building in which she rented a flat belonged to the business and had already been sold to developers. She had been given three months' notice so she wouldn't have to move until March, but what was the point in staying? Jobs in Bristol weren't as plentiful as they were in London, and the latter was much closer to her family. Right now, Juliet wanted to be close to her family. But the happy homecoming they were expecting for the festive season would turn decidedly sour when they heard her news.

They would quickly rally round. She knew that. Her dad would tell her things would soon look up. He had said that the day they moved out of The Grange and he was still saying it, all these years later. Her mum would be genuinely happy to have her back, but sorry for the reason and would offer words of comfort and support, and Zoe would say how wonderful it would be to have her sister home again. The small redundancy package Juliet had been given, together with her meagre savings would see her through for a few months, but not much longer than that. She needed to find a new job, fast. And she didn't have much hope of finding one in Mistletythe, despite it being a busy and seemingly prosperous town. No. London was her best bet. At least it was within commuting distance, even if it did mean over an hour on a train, morning and evening to start with. Once she was settled, she could find a place closer to London in which to live.

Jingle Bells ringing on her phone interrupted Juliet's thoughts. She saw it was her mum calling and forced a smile onto her lips before she answered.

'Hi Mum. I'm less than two minutes away. I'm just about to cross the bridge. If I can actually find it, that is.'

'Hello sweetheart.' Her mum always sounded jolly, no matter how bad things got and merely hearing her voice made the smile spread across Juliet's face. 'Can you believe this weather? Lovely to look at but not quite such fun to venture out in. I hate to ask, but would you be an even bigger sweetheart than you are and pop into Mrs D's for four pints of milk, please? Your father wants cauliflower cheese for supper tonight, followed by blackberry and apple crumble and homemade custard, and we're running low. I know you'll want hot chocolate when you get here. One of us could go but Zoe said you wouldn't mind as you're out anyway.'

Juliet shook her head even though no one could see her. Being in the warmth of her car wasn't quite the same as being "out" but she didn't really mind. If anyone had to freeze to death it might as well be her. 'Of course. Is that all you need?'

'Well, now that I think about it, we may need more butter. And flour too. Zoe and I have been baking. Your favourite cranberry and apple mince pies are in the oven as we speak. Oh, and possibly icing sugar. Hold on a moment sweetheart. Your father's saying he wants something. Bernard, speak up, darling. I'm on the phone.'

'Mum. Why don't you get Zoe to text me a list?' Juliet said, grinning. 'I'll be at Mrs D's in a minute or two but we both know how she always wants to chat, so I'll probably be there for a while.'

'That's an excellent idea, sweetheart. We'll see you very soon. You take care in this weather.'

Juliet ended the handsfree call and peered through the windscreen. Mistletythe Lane, where she was currently parked, led from the town out to the bridge and had no buildings, and no street lights to speak of, just a couple of lampposts dotted here and there. It was about two miles long and was bordered either side by apple orchards, which were actually famous. But not for the apple crop. They were known for their mistletoe which, right now, would be clinging to otherwise bare branches like huge, living Christmas baubles; leathery, evergreen leaves and white pearlescent berries in spherical bunches of varying sizes, for as far as the eye could see. Not that Juliet could see the apple orchards, either. Or the mistletoe. All she could see was snow. And no amount of light would help in such conditions.

She let out a long, loud sigh. She had very little choice. She could either sit in her car and wait, in the hope conditions would improve, or she could take a risk and edge her way across the bridge, to home. The chance of anything coming in the opposite direction was remote, especially at ten-to-five on a Sunday evening … in a blizzard.

She couldn't see so much as a flicker of headlights coming in the opposite direction or hear an engine but she opened her window a fraction to be sure, hurriedly closing it again as snow swirled in along with the bitter cold wind. She turned her wipers off and on again and they made a valiant effort to clear at least a small amount of snow. She let off the handbrake, took a deep breath and gingerly edged forward. She thought she could just make out the line of the stone walls of the bridge but more from memory than sight, she inched her way across, turning off the radio so that she could hear if anything was coming the other way, but all she could hear was the scrunch of virgin snow beneath her tyres.

She breathed a sigh of relief on seeing an amber glow to her left – The Mistletoe pub. That meant she was safely across and was now on Mistletoe Row. In the summer, tables, chairs and benches were set out on the river bank and Juliet had spent many balmy evenings watching swans glide along the sparkling river and bees and butterflies flit around the buddleia, lavender and overhanging weeping willow. Now only the holly bushes would add colour to the pub garden, but even they were hidden by the weather.

Mrs D's, or Dobbie's Convenience Store to give it its full title, also sat to the left, just past the church. It shared a tiny car park at the rear with the pub and the church and oddly enough, the occupants of all three buildings were related. Kevin Dobbie and his second wife, Paula owned and ran The Mistletoe. Noah Waters, Mrs D's brother, was the vicar of St Clement's, and Kevin's parents, Cyril and Myrtle Dobbie owned the store.

Juliet decided to park as close to the shop as she could, which meant pulling up outside and not driving to the car park at the rear. She grabbed her coat from the passenger seat and held it over her head but as she got out and dashed towards the door, the roar of an engine raced towards her. What kind of idiot would be speeding in this weather? The tinkling of the bell above the shop door was superseded by a resounding crack of wing mirrors colliding and Juliet's heart sank a little more, especially as the driver of the other car didn't even attempt to stop.

'That's just great,' she said, closing the door behind her, with a sigh.

'Well, well. Look who the blizzard's blown in.' Mrs D was stacking a shelf with little brown bottles and, placing the final bottle in position she turned to Juliet and grinned. 'Indigestion remedy. It'll be my best seller over the coming days. You mark my words. Would you like one?'

Juliet grinned back, in spite of everything. 'No thanks. I'm good. How are you, Mrs D?'

'Can't complain, dear.' The small, chubby woman shuffled towards her, grey hair pulled tight into a bun which appeared to be stretching her skin taut across high cheek bones and smoothing out some of the mass of wrinkles. She gave Juliet a quick hug. 'How are you, dear Juliet, and where's your Romeo?' Mrs D's eyes crinkled as she chuckled, her rounded shoulders shaking with delight at her regular joke.

'I'm okay thanks. Although I'm not sure I can say the same for my car. Some idiot just clipped my wing mirror. I hope it isn't broken. Anyway. No Romeo, as always.'

'Oh that's a shame.' Mrs D shook her head as she made her way around the shop counter and Juliet wasn't sure if she meant a shame about the wing mirror or Juliet's love life, but Mrs D continued. 'Can you believe this weather? I can't recall the last time we had snow like this. And the bitter cold isn't doing my old bones much good. But there're those far worse off than me. I saw two people sleeping on the streets in Mistletythe last week. Two! What is the world coming to? Probably buried under a blanket of snow right now. Poor souls.' She shook her head again and tutted. 'But we mustn't dwell on such things. It's the festive season and time for happy thoughts. When are you going to find yourself a nice young man and settle down, eh? That's what I'd like to know. You're not getting any younger, dear, and I know it's all the fashion to wait these days, but wait too long and you'll find that ship has sailed. Mark my words. Your ovaries may be as plump as grapes today, but they'll turn to raisins soon enough. Oh it's lovely to see you home again. How long are you staying? Until the New Year?'

Juliet smiled and waited to make sure Mrs D had actually finished. You could never be certain with her.

'I'm not sure,' she said, choosing to ignore the rest and not ready to tell the truth until her own family had heard the news. 'How's Mr D?'

'Bless you for asking, dear. He's the same as ever. Taken up stargazing now, he has. Not that he'll see any in this weather.' She raised her hands in the air and clucked like a chicken. 'Nothing ever holds that man's interest for longer than a month or two. Spent a small fortune on fishing rods, and they're all bundled in the shed. I keep threatening to use them for kindling and you should see the look he gives me.' She rolled her eyes and let out a strange little whistle. 'Now he's ordered some fancy-pantsy telescope. That'll end up in the shed before too long, mark my words.'

'Nothing holds his interest apart from you, Mrs D.' Juliet gave her a wink. 'How long have you been married now? Mum said it's sixty years this year. Is that true?'

Mrs D nodded and a wistful look filled her pale grey eyes. Her thin, rosy-red cheeks puffed out and a tender smile spread across pink lips. 'Sixty years on Boxing Day. And never a night apart in all that time, dear. I wish you could find a man like my Cyril. That's what you need. A man to cherish you and love you, no matter what.' She returned Juliet's wink and leant her forearms on the only space on the counter not covered with newspapers and magazines.

Juliet glanced at her phone as the tinkle of a text alert let her know her mum's list had arrived. She gave it a quick look and scrolled down to the end. It was some list. Juliet smiled at Mrs D. 'A man is the last thing I need, Mrs D, but I do need quite a few things for Mum. Will you point me in the direction of baking foil, please?'

The shop might be small but every inch of it, from floor to ceiling, was jam-packed with stock and, just like the supermarkets, Mrs D liked to move things around.

'It's in the back, right hand corner, dear. Next to the kitchen roll.' Mrs D pointed in that general direction.

'Excellent. I've got to get kitchen roll too.'

Juliet wandered around the shop, loading her basket while Mrs D filled her in on all the local gossip, most of which either Zoe or her mum had already told her. But Mrs D loved a good gossip and Juliet oohed and aahed as necessary. When she finally approached the counter, checking the list on her phone to make sure she had got everything, Mrs D made an odd little coughing sound.

'He's coming back this year, dear.'

'Who? Dan?' Juliet grinned at her. 'He comes back every year at some stage over the holidays. I thought you'd finally given up trying to get your grandson and me together.'

'I wasn't talking about Daniel.' Mrs D's tone didn't sound quite as cheery as it had.

'Oh? Then who?' But even before Mrs D said the words, Juliet somehow knew. Her chest tightened, her mouth became dry, goosebumps prickled her skin. It was as if she were having an allergic reaction. And in a way, she was.

'Harrison Bow.' Mrs D's voice was merely a whisper.

'Harrison?' Juliet's phone slid from her fingers as she stared at Mrs D. Thankfully, it landed in a box filled with tinsel at Juliet's feet but it was a moment or two before she bent down to retrieve it. She looked directly at Mrs D. 'You're mistaken, surely?' Twenty years ago, Harrison Bow had sworn he'd never set foot on Mistletoe Row again, or visit his grandfather at The Grange, and as far as Juliet knew, he hadn't. Why would he come back after all this time? Unless? 'Is the old man ill?'

'Not that I know, dear. That old crook will outlive the lot of us, you mark my words. No. It's something to do with young Luke, I believe.'

'Has something happened to Luke?' Luke was Harrison's younger brother. And possibly the only person in the world Harrison actually cared about.

Mrs D threw her a curious look. 'Why must something have happened to someone to make Harrison return? He's a grown man now and an extremely successful one from all we've heard. Perhaps he wants to make amends. Put the past behind him.'

'Or perhaps he's coming to check up on his inheritance. To make sure he's still going to get everything.'

'I doubt that very much, dear. And if so, why now? Old Bow isn't likely to change his will after all these years. If he was ever going to disinherit Harrison, he would've done it twenty years ago, when the lad walked out.'

'I still don't believe he did walk out. I think he ran away because he wasn't man enough to face me. I mean, face everyone.'

'I don't know, dear. From what I heard, he and his grandad had the row to end all rows. After his head-to-head with you, of course. But none of us really knew him, did we?' Mrs D had a faraway look in her eye for a moment. 'I wonder if he's changed. You still look the same as you did all those years ago. That wonderful strawberry-blonde hair, those freckles and that determined gleam in your hazel eyes. Just like your mother's.' She smiled affectionately at Juliet before her brows furrowed. 'Although they aren't quite so filled with fire as they were. He was a scrawny teenager, if I remember rightly. But good-looking, in a moody sort of way. The complete opposite of young Luke. Harrison was so serious, wasn't he? Not that he was here for long. But he certainly made a lasting impression.' She pulled a face and nodded sagely. 'We weren't likely to forget Harrison Bow in a hurry.'

Hardly a hurry. It was twenty years ago. But Mrs D was right. Harrison had definitely made his mark. Mostly for all the wrong reasons. Juliet often thought she was the only one who really remembered him, but of course she wasn't. Everyone who lived on Mistletoe Row twenty years ago would remember him.

No one would forget what happened.

Least of all, Juliet.

Chapter Two

The wipers of Harrison's Mercedes GLS glided across the windscreen as they batted away large flakes of snow. At least he'd avoided the earlier blizzard. Now the snow was falling far more gently and whilst visibility on the roads wasn't great, it was a lot better than it had been. He was glad he had delayed his journey by several hours, even though it meant arriving in the dark, and late into the evening. That was a bonus, in fact. He would only need to spend an hour or so with his grandfather before the old man retired to his room for the night. Harrison may not have set foot inside The Grange for twenty years, but he knew exactly what went on there. Luke made sure of that.

And Luke wasn't Harrison's only informant. Three years ago, Rufus Bow, who was ninety this year, had begrudgingly agreed to a live-in housekeeper to oversee the day-to-day running of the house. A housekeeper paid for by Harrison.

Not that Rufus could say no. The house belonged to Harrison, not to Rufus, and had done so for the last eight years, despite what everyone else might think. In fact, strictly speaking, it had belonged to Harrison since the day it was purchased from the Bells; he simply hadn't known about it at the time. More than once during the last eight years, Harrison had been sorely tempted to tell the old man to leave, but he never had. He might detest his grandfather, but family was family, no matter what he may have done.

'So this is Mistletythe,' Kiki, Harrison's executive assistant said, peering out at the snow-laden streets of the town. 'I see what you mean by "quiet". The place is bordering on dead.'

She threw him a smile and he smiled back. 'I warned you, so it's too late to blame me. I still don't know why you wanted to come.' He glanced from side to side. 'The place hasn't changed in twenty years.'

Kiki twisted in her seat and tipped her head to one side, a curtain of sleek, mahogany hair falling to her elbows. 'Why haven't you been back for twenty years? Did you ever tell me? I can't recall.'

He hadn't, and she knew it. So what was she playing at, exactly? He'd never spoken of that time to her or to anyone since it happened; since he'd vowed never to return to The Grange, or to ever drive along Mistletoe Row again – the scene of one of the unhappiest times of his life.

'No. And I'm not going to tell you now, so forget it. One thing I will say though, is beware of the old man. He may be ninety but all his faculties are intact. And he can be a real charmer when it suits him. He can make you believe in unicorns if he wants to.'

'Unicorns?' Kiki gave a ripple of laughter and pulled a face at him. 'Where did that come from? I've never heard you mention unicorns before.'

Harrison cursed under his breath. He hadn't even got to Mistletoe Row and already that damn girl was playing on his mind. Twenty years had passed and yet still Juliet bloody Bell and her sodding unicorns were the first thing that popped into his head the moment he was within spitting distance of the place.

'It's something someone once said about me and my grandfather. What I'm saying is, don't believe everything he tells you. In fact, don't believe anything. That way you stand less chance of getting hurt.'

'Getting hurt? Jesus, Harrison. What's come over you? You're acting weird. You've been acting weird since the day your brother called and asked you to come down here for Christmas. If you didn't want to come, why are we here?'

He tightened his grip on the steering wheel and clenched his teeth.

'Harrison?' Kiki coaxed.

'I'm here because Luke asked me to be. You're here because you said you had nowhere else to go this year and you might as well come with me and get paid double-time.' He threw her a sardonic smile.

'Double my Christmas bonus, I believe you mentioned.' She laid a manicured hand on his forearm and grinned. 'And it's not that I didn't have anywhere else to go. You're well aware that I could be skiing in Aspen with Charlie and the crowd. I chose to be here with you.'

He cast a quick glance in her direction and furrowed his brows. 'Why was that? I told you it wouldn't be fun. Or festive. Or anything else you're expecting. I told you it would be all work, in a dark and dingy old house and that you'd be far better off going to Aspen with your brother. And yet here you are. And you say I'm the one who's acting weird.'

Kiki let out a little sigh. 'Let's just say, I fancied a change. And I like spending time with you. You know that. We're friends first, more than we are boss and assistant, aren't we? We've been friends for years, yet we've never spent Christmas, or any other holiday time together. I thought it would be nice if we did.'

He raised one brow. 'So you said when you told me you wanted to come. I don't think spending holiday time with one's boss is a requisite for a good working relationship, Kiki, or something friends need to do. In fact, I think it would be quite the opposite in many cases.'

'But we're not like other people, are we? We have something special, don't you think?'

She twisted a lock of her hair around her finger and Harrison watched her from the corner of his eye. He couldn't decide if she was going for sexy, or petulant. Her tone was soft and sultry but the expression on her undeniably beautiful face was more like a spoilt child.

'We certainly work well together,' he said, turning his attention to the road and changing the subject. 'You can't see them, due to the fact that the local council is too mean to install adequate street lighting, but we're now on Mistletythe Lane and it's bordered either side by apple orchards. This time of year the apple trees are laden with bunches of mistletoe. Did you know that mistletoe is a parasitic plant and attaches itself to a host? Although it doesn't actually kill the host tree, just lives off its nutrients. It's a bit like some members of my family, in that respect.' He flashed Kiki a meaningful grin.

She grinned back. 'Or like an alien from another planet.'

'My relatives, or the plant?' He raised a brow before continuing: 'It also grows on lime and hawthorn in the UK, and poplar and conifer, I believe. Although I'm no expert. It's spread by birds. They eat the berries and wipe their beaks on the branches of the trees, leaving the mistletoe seed behind to establish itself. Or perhaps it's in their poop. Anyway, it takes years for it to get to the stage where it can bear berries. But Mistletoe is more valuable than the apple crop around here, which is why the mistletoe has been encouraged to thrive. It's a shame you won't get to see it. Even in daylight it'll be hidden under all this snow.'

'We're going to be here for a week or two, aren't we? You never know what might happen.'

For some reason, Harrison wasn't sure she was still talking about the mistletoe but he ignored the comment as he reached the narrow bridge and they drove across it in silence. From here, Mistletoe Row was full of twists and turns as it wound its way for about a mile until it climbed up Mistletoe Mount on which the stately Georgian house, The Grange, stood proud at the top, overlooking the clutch of cottages, the church, the pub and Dobbie's Convenience Store.

'At least there's a pub,' Kiki said, nodding to her left.

'And a church,' Harrison said, grinning. 'Not that you've probably ever been inside one of those, have you?'

Kiki tutted and pouted her bright red lips. 'I'll have you know, Harrison Bow that I was a Catholic convent school girl. I spent more years than I care to remember inside a church.'

'I'm impressed. I didn't know that about you.'

'There're a lot of things you don't know about me, Harrison. And there are lots of things I don't know about you, despite the fact that you and

Charlie have been friends for at least ten years. We can spend this holiday finding out.'

He didn't like the sound of that. It came across as more of a threat than a treat. Or perhaps that was just him being his usual stand-off self and putting up his barriers. Maybe it was time he stopped doing that? After all, he was back on Mistletoe Row for the first time in twenty years, wasn't he? And hadn't Luke begged him to come and to try to put the past behind him? Behind them all. Perhaps the time was right. Kiki was drop-dead gorgeous and he was pretty sure she liked him. Perhaps spending this Christmas with her by his side wouldn't be all bad. Even if he would also be spending it with his grandfather.

He tried not to look at number 29 as he passed, but he couldn't quite stop his head from turning briefly in that direction. The cottage looked warm, cosy and welcoming on the outside with its rows of white fairy lights, a garland of holly and mistletoe above the double front door and an amber glow from every window. Inside, he could imagine it would be even more festive, warm and welcoming. But not to him. If he knocked on that door, it'd be slammed in his face a second after it was opened. They'd probably toss out a bunch of garlic, and possibly even some holy water, for good measure. One of the last things Juliet Bell had said to him was that he was a bloodsucking pariah. Before she'd wished him dead. He hadn't forgotten that. Even after twenty years.

'Is that it?'

For a second Harrison wondered if Kiki could read his thoughts. Until he realised she was staring in the direction of Mistletoe Mount and The Grange.

'Yep. That's it. It looks bloody depressing, doesn't it?'

She met his eyes. 'It could definitely do with a bit of brightening up. Doesn't your grandad, or your brother like Christmas? God! The place does have electricity, doesn't it? I can't see one light anywhere. Perhaps everyone's gone out?'

Harrison laughed mirthlessly. 'The old man will no doubt be in his study at the back of the house, and if I know Luke, he'll be in the gym, or the indoor pool, both also at the back. Daphne, the live-in housekeeper is probably in the kitchen.'

'Also at the back, I suppose,' Kiki said, raising perfectly arched brows. 'What's at the front?'

'The sitting room, dining room, library and my study.'

'Your study? But you told me you haven't been here for twenty years.'

'I haven't. When the old man bought the place – and I use that word charitably – he gave me a study. I know for a fact that's exactly as it was. And nothing will have changed because that old man will never change. That's simply the way he is.'

'You really don't like him, do you? What did he do to make you hate him so?'

Harrison sneered. 'What did he do? He ruined my life. And not just my life, but other people's too.'

'Ruined your life?' Kiki's brows shot together and her voice increased by at least an octave. 'If this is your life ruined, I can't imagine just how wonderful it was before. God, Harrison. People would kill to have your life. And that includes me.'

He shot her a look and after a moment he nodded. 'I suppose you're right. And it wasn't that my life was wonderful before. But it could've been. It could've been the sort of life people only dream about. He made sure that could never be.'

'Will you ever tell me about it?'

Her voice was soft and soothing but when she laid a hand on his knee, he moved his leg away.

'Sorry, Kiki. I'm behaving like a bloody jerk, I know. It's this place. Seeing it again after all these years has brought it all back with a vengeance. But I'm being melodramatic. Ignore me. I expect you're beginning to regret offering to join me for Christmas, aren't you?'

'Absolutely not. I'm looking forward to it. I can't wait to see Luke again. It must be several months since he visited you. And I'm dying to meet your grandad in spite of everything you've said about him. Or not said, to be more precise. I think this is the most you've spoken of him since

I've known you, and certainly since I started working for you four years ago.'

'Four years? Has it only been four? It feels a lot longer than that.'

'Thanks.' She playfully tapped his arm. 'I'll take that as a compliment.'

He grinned. 'You should. It was meant as one. You've become a good friend, Kiki. More like a sister, in fact.'

'Great.' She folded her arms and pouted.

'What's wrong with that?' He stopped the car outside the front door of The Grange and turned to her and smiled.

'You should've stopped at good friend.' She twisted in her seat and met his eyes. 'I don't want to be your sister, Harrison. I want…'

The front door of The Grange burst open and Kiki's voice trailed off as Harrison looked away to see his younger brother dashing towards them.

Chapter Three

Juliet still hadn't told her family about her redundancy despite having been home for more than three hours. She had meant to do so once all the exuberant greetings were over but her mum insisted she should take a lovely, long bath before supper and the prospect of soaking in scented bubbles far outweighed her need to break her news.

'You must be frozen to the core,' her mum had said, the minute Juliet struggled in via the back door with the bags of shopping in her hands and her holdall slung across her shoulder, accompanied by a rather large flurry of snow and a gust of wind that sent the curtains flapping. 'I can hardly see you under the layers of snow. I hadn't realised how bad it was out there.'

'Good heavens, sweetheart,' her dad had added, swooping forward and slamming the back door shut. 'Let me take those bags. Was the journey dreadful? Of course it was. What with the delays you called and told us about, and this dreadful weather. Sometimes I forget a conversation I've just had.' He took the shopping bags and chuckled as he placed them on the kitchen table.

'Chuck me your coat,' Zoe said, rolling her eyes as Juliet removed the holdall and dropped it at her feet. 'You'll be thawing out all over the kitchen floor and I've already mopped the thing three times today. Good to have you home though. Want a glass of mulled wine?'

Juliet laughed as she regained her breath after battling her way up the garden path. She shrugged off her coat, handed it to Zoe and then hugged each member of her family in turn, even Cinnamon, who had woken up and come to greet her.

'Yes please to the wine, Zoe. And I'd love a hot bath, Mum, if you don't mind. I'm absolutely shattered.'

'Mind? Why would I mind? We can chat when you're warm and dry. We don't want you getting hypothermia. Zoe and I will make supper. You go and relax, sweetheart.'

Juliet didn't need telling twice. She had more things in the car but they could stay there until morning. Everything she needed was in her holdall and her family wouldn't mind if she ate supper dressed in her PJs, dressing gown and slippers. The kitchen smelt divine, the cottage was cosy and she was more than a little relieved to be home. The bad news could wait.

She had fully intended to bring the subject up over supper, but the truth was, since leaving Mrs D's she had thought of little else but Harrison Bow. Why would he return after all these years? What could Luke have said to bring him home? Did her family know? They hadn't mentioned it to her and surely they knew it was something she should be told? Or perhaps that was precisely why they hadn't done so? Perhaps they thought she might not come home for Christmas if she discovered there was a chance she would bump into him.

No one had mentioned him as they consumed the cauliflower cheese and baked beans, either. Or the blackberry and apple crumble with homemade custard. All her family talked about was the weather, how good it was to have her home and whether she felt up to getting the Christmas tree in the morning now that the blizzard had subsided. That led into a long conversation about when, exactly, her dad planned to go into the roof space and bring down the decorations because apparently he had been promising to do so all week, and hadn't. Which in turn led into a discussion about the possibility of buying some new decorations this year. As usual, a question relating to the family finances sent her dad scurrying off to his study like a scared rabbit.

'I'll leave that up to you, dear hearts,' he said. 'There are a few things I need to do this evening. You don't mind if I leave you for an hour or two, do you?' He didn't wait for a reply, before disappearing with his coffee for the remainder of the evening.

It was as if a cloud descended. No sooner had her dad scampered than her mum said she had some presents to wrap for the Women's Institute meeting the following evening and if Juliet didn't mind, she would go and do that now so that tomorrow would be completely free.

A second or two later, Zoe told Juliet she was shattered.

'It's been a really long day, sis and I fell over this afternoon when I was walking Cinnamon. I'm fine,' she said, gesturing stop with her hand before Juliet asked the question. 'Every bone in my body is aching now though. I think a long, hot bath is actually what I need. Would you mind if we caught up in the morning? You could probably do with an early night after your journey anyway.' She simply smiled as she rose to leave and gave Juliet another quick hug before dashing into the hall.

Juliet let out a little sigh. 'Well, Cinnamon. It looks like it's just you and me.'

Cinnamon raised her head a fraction, one long, red furry ear flopping across one eye before letting out a louder sigh than Juliet's and dropping her head back to the floor as if it was all too much effort. That was followed by a brief trumpeting sound and a smell like rotten eggs permeated the scent of spices lingering in the air.

'Cinnamon!' Juliet screwed up her face and waved her hand in front of her nose to try to bat away the awful smell.

Cinnamon smacked her jaws together a few times, stretched out one paw and made a self-satisfied, rumbling whine of contentment from deep within her throat.

'Thanks. What a great homecoming this is turning out to be.'

Juliet glanced at the clock on the kitchen wall, festooned with sprigs of holly and mistletoe. At half past eight on a Sunday night in Bristol, she would be curled up in front of the TV watching some drama or other on the BBC, a bowl of Marks and Spencer winter berries and prosecco crisps on the side table together with a bottle of prosecco to wash them down. If she searched the cupboards, she would probably find both, and if she kept the volume low on the TV in the sitting room, she wouldn't disturb her family. But somehow the thought of it made her feel even more melancholy than she had earlier. To be alone in her flat watching TV was one thing. To be in a warm and cosy cottage surrounded by her family, and to do that, was a different thing entirely.

She got up and wandered into the dining room. The antique mahogany table still looked incongruous in here; and that was without its extension leaves. In the dining room of The

Grange, it had looked perfect and had room to spare even with the three extensions added and surrounded by thirty matching chairs. Here, if they had guests, everyone had to breathe in to squeeze between the walls and the backs of the eight chairs they'd brought with them.

Now, with the chairs pushed in she could walk to the window – but she soon wished she hadn't. From here she had a clear view of Mistletoe Park, across the road from the cottage. It had once belonged to The Grange but was sold off over one hundred years ago and was now common land, managed by the local council. The massive Christmas tree with its myriad coloured lights stood at one end, opposite the church, and she could see the glow in the dark, though not the tree itself.

If she turned her head to the left, she could see Mistletoe Mount at the other end of the park. At the top stood The Grange and although she told herself not to, she couldn't stop from looking up at the house she and her family had once called home. And possibly still would, if it hadn't been for Harrison Bow and his grandad.

The house reflected her mood as she stared at it. Not one light could be seen. It looked cold, forbidding and depressing. She could only make out the shape of it in the darkness but she still knew every inch of it – unless the Bows had changed it, of course. She had been told they hadn't, but who knew with that lot? Every word they spoke was a lie. Perhaps they'd ripped out its ancient heart of oak, plus the later Georgian additions and painted everything white, modernising it all.

In the days the Bells lived there, the place shone out like a beacon. The wood floors were polished until you could almost see your own reflection, the fires in every room were lit, the lights burned bright from dusk till dawn and the windows glowed with a warm welcome. This time of year, every tree within fifty feet of the house would have been dressed in fairy lights, together with a massive Christmas tree, or two. Candle lanterns were lit in the drive. A large wreath hung on the doors which were surrounded by boughs of pine entwined with holly and mistletoe. Cars would queue to park outside as guests of the family piled into the cosy interior, looking forward to all the forthcoming festivities. Food and drink would flow as easily as the conversations; games would be played, carols sung; long walks taken on frosty mornings in the woods behind the house; ice skating on the lake in the grounds; and on Boxing Day, they would ride their horses and the antique carriages through the park.

Even after twenty years, Juliet missed it all so much it hurt. She had been able to keep her own horse, Morning Star, for a while, though he was long since dead. The rest, together with the carriages and virtually everything else apart from a few items of furniture and personal family possessions, had been sold with The Grange and what remained of the estate after centuries of dwindling funds in the Bell family's coffers.

The tail lights of a car were approaching The Grange and she peered at them in the distance as the vehicle came to a halt. The hall light went on and a shaft of yellow beamed onto the drive as the front door burst open. The Grange was little more than the size of a doll's house from where she stood but she could see someone running towards the car in the beam of light and two more people getting out of it. Just black stick figures silhouetted in the darkness and the light.

Her heartbeat quickened as she watched them and when she brushed a lock of hair from her face, a river of ice ran through her.

Was one of those people Harrison Bow?

Chapter Four

'You're here!'

'Damn,' Harrison said, getting out of the car and grinning at his exuberant young brother. 'I knew I'd taken the wrong turning. I was hoping to be in New York.'

'Yeah, yeah.' Luke bear hugged him.

'Been working out?' Harrison raised an eyebrow and looked Luke up and down, holding him at arm's length now. Luke spent every spare hour in the gym or in the pool. Appearance meant a great deal to him. It still amazed Harrison how different they were. Harrison couldn't care less about such things.

Luke shrugged nonchalantly and grinned. 'Oh, you know. You should try it bro. You're getting on a bit now. You don't want to end up like the old man.'

Harrison stiffened at the mention of their grandfather but he continued the friendly banter.

'Not so much of it, kid. Thirty-eight is the new eighteen. Haven't you heard? Which makes you about five. So say hello to Kiki and run along like a good boy and tell Daphne we're here.'

Luke's grin broadened. 'I told her the minute I heard your car.' He tipped his head to one side and smiled at Kiki. 'Hi Kiki. Welcome to the dungeon. It's a jolly place, as you can see. We don't have any staff other than Daphne and a couple of people who do the cleaning. Oh, and a gardener. But Daphne's the only one here at this time of the night, so if you need a hand with your bags, it'll have to be mine.'

Kiki smiled. 'Hi, Luke. I can manage, thanks.'

'That Merc sounds like it's on its last legs, too,' Luke said, returning his attention to Harrison. 'Isn't it time you traded it in for a new one?'

Harrison opened the boot and handed a plain black leather holdall to Luke. 'It's a vintage Mercedes. You don't trade in vintage cars for new ones. Haven't you learnt anything from all your years living here with the old man?' He grabbed a second matching holdall which he threw over his shoulder along with Kiki's Louis Vuitton one and put her matching suitcase on the ground, extending the handle before grabbing his laptop bag and handing it to Luke. 'Guard that with your life.' A moment later they all headed towards the house.

'Most people don't drive their vintage cars around in the snow.' Luke gave him a mock look of disapproval.

'Ah. So you have learnt something. You believe things of value should be hidden from sight and only brought out to show off to everyone before being locked away again. I don't follow that philosophy. I believe if you own something lovely you should enjoy it.'

Luke peered around Harrison and grinned at Kiki. 'Did you enjoy the drive down here? I bet you'd have preferred to be in my brand new BMW, wouldn't you?'

'Not with you at the wheel, no.' She threw him a smile. 'Where is it?'

He gave a bark of laughter and darted a look at Harrison. 'Locked away in the garage. But only because it was such a fantastic present from my big bro and I want to look after it.'

Harrison tutted. 'You've crashed it already, haven't you? How long did that take? You've only had it for five weeks.'

Luke shoved the front door further open with his backside and frowned. 'I haven't crashed it.'

Harrison raised his brows. 'Really?'

'Yes. Really. It's in the garage because of this weather. Snow does untold damage to paintwork you know.' Luke put the holdall on the floor and sighed. 'Oh, okay. But it's only a tiny scratch. Hardly visible, in fact. And it happened today. Because I was rushing to be back here in time for your arrival. I thought you'd get here around five, not well after eight. Some idiot had parked outside

Dobbie's and the wing mirror caught mine as I drove by.'

Harrison shook his head. 'Don't you mean you hit the wing mirror of the other car as you sped past? I assume you stopped to check if you'd done any damage to their vehicle?'

'In this weather? It was during the blizzard we had earlier and I'd gone past before I realised. Anyway, I only clipped it so at worst, it'll have a tiny scratch, like mine. Hardly worth exchanging insurance details for that.'

'But worth offering to pay for the repair, if necessary. God, Luke. Don't turn out like the old man and think you can just breeze through life and run over anyone or anything that gets in your way.'

'I don't. And I'm nothing like Grandfather, believe me. I didn't think, that's all. I was in a rush and it's not the first time I've clipped wing mirrors. It never causes much damage.'

'Even so. Did you recognise the car? Was it someone local?'

'I could hardly see it in the blizzard. But if it'll make you happy, I'll ask around tomorrow and if I find out whose car it was, I'll offer to pay for the damage. Okay?'

'Good. Ah, Daphne. Hello. How are you?'

'Good evening, Harrison. I'm well, thank you. And yourself?'

'Fine thanks. This is Kiki, my assistant. And friend,' he added as he walked towards the ornate, central staircase. 'Which room have you allocated? I may as well take the bags up straight away.'

'The Rose room.' Daphne turned and smiled at Kiki. 'I hope you like it. It's one of the most feminine and has a beautiful view over the rose gardens at the side of the house and down towards the park. No roses at this time of year of course, but the winter bedding is always colourful although due to all this snow, you can't even see that at the moment. But the room gets the early evening light and it's bright and cosy. It's also close to Harrison's and I thought, as you're here working, you'd want to be nearby.'

'Absolutely. Thank you, Daphne,' Kiki said. 'I'm sure I'll love it.'

'The Rose room?' Harrison hesitated for a milli-second, halfway up the stairs. 'No, that's fine. Follow me, Kiki and I'll show you.'

She hurried after him and as they turned right at the top of the stairs and walked along the hall, she said, 'Oh wow. They've all got little paintings below the names. And such pretty writing. Which room is yours? Or does it have 'Harrison's room. Keep out' and a painting of a skull and crossbones or something below it?'

He grinned at her and nodded at a door with the words, 'Lake room' in beautiful, calligraphic handwriting, above a tiny painting of a lake. 'That's mine. It overlooks the lake, oddly enough.'

They also passed 'Sundown room' before they reached Kiki's, and Harrison waited for her to ask.

'Whose room is that one?'

'Luke's.'

'So where's your grandad's room?'

'At the other end of the house. He's in the 'Twilight room'. Which is actually quite apt in so many ways.'

'And Daphne's?'

'Willow room. It overlooks a willow bed. But they're not all named for their view. Some, like the Floral room, are named for the internal decoration.'

'Fascinating.'

He grinned at her. 'You mean boring. But it's better than having a number on each door, and with twenty bedrooms, it could easily get confusing.' He opened her bedroom door and switched on the light and then, almost to himself added, 'I'd forgotten how beautiful this is.'

'Twenty bedrooms? I didn't realise it was so big, even though it looks it from the outside. Your grandad must be loaded to keep this place going.'

'What? Oh yes. It certainly isn't cheap. I'll leave you to get settled in, but you won't have long. Luke wanted us to have dinner with him and that'll be at nine. Hopefully, the old man will have eaten earlier so he'll only join us for a drink beforehand, and he'll go off to his room. Come downstairs as soon as you're ready. Let Daphne know if there's anything you need.'

Kiki smiled and glanced around the room as she entered. 'Wow. I feel as if I've stepped back in time. I should've brought a flapper dress and long strings of pearls. Is there an en suite?'

'No need to look so panicked.' He walked towards one of the walls which were covered in hand-painted, rambling roses and pushed one of the rose buds. A door swung open revealing a fully equipped, relatively modern bathroom, along with a claw-foot, bath. 'The en suites were added in the early nineteen hundreds and several were hidden like this one. Purely for aesthetic reasons. Prior to that there were more bedrooms, but many were divided up to form the en suites. Most have been updated recently. See you downstairs.' He smiled at her and left.

Only as he went into his own room and took in the sheer beauty of it did he realise that Kiki hadn't said she liked her room. His boasted intricately carved woodwork, ornate ceiling, antique light fittings, large, Georgian windows and original shutters. And the Rose room was one of the prettiest in the house. In fact, it had been Juliet's room when she and her family had lived at The Grange. He could remember her telling him that she loved the view over the park, down to the church, and the river, the old stone bridge, and the apple orchards beyond.

His fists clenched unwittingly and he could feel the tightness in his jaw. He should've had a word with Daphne about the rooms. He shouldn't have allowed Kiki to have that one.

He cursed himself under his breath. He was being ridiculous. It was a room, not a living, breathing thing with feelings and memories. The room wouldn't care who slept in it and Juliet would never know.

Even if by some chance they bumped into one another while he was here, they were hardly likely to discuss The Grange. They were hardly likely to discuss anything. They weren't on speaking terms. They hadn't spoken for twenty years.

But if, by some miracle they did, would Juliet be likely to admit she had been wrong? And could he, even after all this time, forgive and forget the things she said?

He dumped his bags on the floor, shrugged off his coat, slung it over an armchair and turned to head back downstairs. Why was he even thinking about Juliet bloody Bell? He was obviously tired. What he needed was a drink or two, and a good meal. Followed, perhaps, by a game of billiards with Luke.

He shot a glance at the closed door of the Rose room before marching down the stairs. Perhaps one of the other bedrooms could be made up. After all, Kiki didn't seem exactly thrilled by the room. She might prefer to be in one of the others.

He'd have a word with Daphne and see.

Chapter Five

Merry's Christmas Tree Farm was on the outskirts of Michaelmas Bay, a town fifteen miles or so away, but Juliet and her family felt it was well worth the trip, even in such snowy conditions. Besides, it was much milder this morning. Unseasonably warm, according to the radio presenter. The clouds had dissipated, the sun was shining and the snow was already starting to thaw as they drove to the farm at ten that morning. This was where they had purchased their tree every year since Robin Merry, the youngest son of arable farmers, Ashley and Ava Merry, had run the Christmas tree farm.

Robin began it as a sideline when he was a young boy and word of mouth ensured that his popularity had grown, year on year. He sold the trees from one particular field at the entrance to the main farm and a wooden sign went up the moment

Merry's Christmas Tree Farm was open for business, usually in the second week of December.

A few years ago, Robin converted a shepherd's hut and made it look like an igloo on the outside. Inside, sheepskin rugs lay on a dark wood floor and in one corner a large cast iron pot containing mulled wine, simmered on a wood burning stove. There was a wooden bench and a small table, plus several large, comfy cushions scattered around the floor, with Christmas-themed curtains at the windows and the front door. It looked more like one of those upmarket glamping places than it did his office-cum-shop, and Juliet was pleased to see it hadn't changed since last year.

'Merry Christmas,' Robin said, beaming at Juliet and her family as they pulled up outside his office and got out of her dad's car. His Santa hat sat lopsided on a shock of hair the colour of golden treacle which framed his ruddy complexion. 'Lovely to see you again, Rosa, Bernard, Zoe and Juliet. The snow's a bit deep today but I've picked out a few trees I thought you might like. If you don't want one of those though, feel free to take a walk around.'

One of the reasons Robin was so popular was that he seemed to have a knack of, not only remembering all his customers by name, but also exactly what they were looking for, even though he only saw many of them once a year, during December.

'Thanks, Robin,' Bernard said. 'Nice to see you too.'

A girl appeared with a tray bearing mugs of mulled wine. She wore a matching Santa hat on her jet-black hair but her complexion was porcelain-white. Her smile was as warm and welcoming as Robin's as she handed out the drinks. 'Merry Christmas. Perfect weather to buy a tree.'

'This is my girlfriend, Raven Starr,' Robin said. 'Her grandparents own Snowflake Inn in Snowflake Cove.'

'I've been there,' Zoe said, taking one of the mugs and smiling at Raven. 'It's a lovely place. Didn't Zachary Thorn do a Christmas Special of his TV show, 'Thorn On Your Side' from there last year?'

'Yep,' Raven said, passing a mug to Juliet. 'He's dating my aunt, Evie Starr. He virtually lives there now.'

'Wow. Lucky Evie. He's gorgeous.' Zoe shot a look at Juliet and winked at Raven. 'Does he have a brother?'

'Afraid not. Are you looking for a boyfriend?'

Zoe shook her head. 'Not me, no. But my sister is.'

Juliet's mouth fell open. 'No, I'm not. A man is the last thing I need right now.'

Raven grinned at Juliet. 'Just a tree then?'

'Yes. But if you know anyone who wants a sister, I've got one going spare.'

'Let me show you the trees I've selected,' Robin said, smiling.

Rosa took the mug Raven offered, but Bernard shook his head. 'Not for me, thank you, Raven. I'm driving and the roads aren't sufficiently gritted. I'd better not take a chance. Better to be safe than sorry.'

'I can make you a coffee, or a hot chocolate if you like.'

'That's very kind. But I'll be fine, thanks.' Bernard smiled at Raven and he and Rosa followed Robin to a row of trees leaning against the fence to his left.

'Looks like you've got more customers,' Zoe said, giving Juliet an odd look as another car came up the drive.

'Excuse me,' Raven said. 'I'd better welcome them while Robin's with your dad, and get some more mulled wine. Want this one?' She held out the mug that Bernard had declined.

'Absolutely,' Zoe said, almost snatching the mug from her and emptying the contents into her own. 'Thanks.'

Raven grinned. 'You're welcome.' She took the empty mug and headed towards the approaching car.

'Oh look,' Zoe said. 'I do believe that's Luke's car. Luke Bow.' She knocked back the contents of her mug as Juliet stared at her.

'Luke Bow?' Juliet struggled to say the name. 'What the hell is he doing here?'

Zoe shook her head as the car pulled up. 'This place is popular. I suppose Luke's here to get a tree, just like we are. But who on earth is that gorgeous man with him?'

Juliet forced herself to look and immediately regretted it.

It may have been twenty years since she had seen that face, but she would recognise it no matter how much time had passed. It may be more muscular, the jaw firmer, the mouth more defined, framed by hair a darker shade of chestnut and expertly cut, but it was *him*. Broader, taller and far more rugged-looking than he was at eighteen and still oozing sex appeal even from several metres away. He was immaculately and expensively dressed, just as he had been at eighteen. He was helping what must have been the most beautiful woman in the world, get out of the car. She seemed to have got her heel stuck and they were both laughing as he bent down to free it and then she tossed a length of super-shiny mahogany hair over her shoulder as she linked her arm through his and they walked forward.

'I told you not to wear heels,' he said, shaking his head but smiling at the beautiful woman.

Even his voice was the same, but perhaps slightly deeper pitched.

Juliet's chest felt as if it was in a vice and her heart pumped so hard she was certain everyone must be able to hear its thumping beat. The butterflies in her stomach and weakness in her knees were the same as they had been the very first time she had seen him.

He glanced in Juliet's direction and looked away.

And then he shot a look back again.

His mouth opened a fraction.

He stopped in his tracks.

'Juliet?' he said, as if he'd seen a ghost and didn't quite believe it.

Juliet said nothing. She couldn't find her voice. But his eyes looked a richer shade of coffee-brown as she met his stare.

'Well, well,' Luke said. Not that Juliet had even noticed him until he spoke. 'This is a small world.'

Chapter Six

Juliet perched on the arm of the chair in which her mum Rosa sat with a large box of Christmas decorations resting on her lap. Zoe stood opposite and Rosa handed decorations to each of them in turn to hang on the beautiful Norway Spruce that they, together with Bernard, had manhandled into a large red pot less than an hour earlier and dragged in front of the sitting room window. It had taken them more time to decide on the perfect position of the tree than it had to select it. But perhaps one of the reasons that the selection hadn't taken long was the fact that Harrison and Luke Bow had turned up at Merry's Christmas Tree Farm. Along with the most beautiful woman in the world. A fact that had irritated Juliet almost as much as coming face-to-face with the one man in the world she hated.

'I still can't believe you walked away and sat in the car without saying one word,' Zoe said, hanging a silver and white painted glass bauble on a branch.

Juliet scowled as she took another bauble from her mum. 'And I still don't believe their arrival was as much of a surprise to you as it was to me. But as I said in the car, I don't want to discuss it.'

'What are you saying, sweetheart?' Rosa asked. 'Are you suggesting Zoe had something to do with them arriving at the exact same time as we were there?'

'Yes. That's exactly what I'm saying. She didn't seem surprised at all. But she did seem nervous. As if she knew something was going to happen that might end in disaster.'

'Oh come on,' Zoe said. 'Two people bumping into one another after not seeing each other for twenty years is hardly a disaster, is it? Some people might say it was a good thing. A chance to put the past behind them.'

Juliet glowered at her. 'Some people would be wrong. And it may not have been a disaster from where you stood, but believe me, from my shoes, it was a total nightmare. And one I sincerely hope won't be repeated.'

'Where's your Christmas spirit? Isn't it supposed to be the season of goodwill to all men?'

'All men apart from Harrison Bow. And his grandad.'

Zoe shook her head. 'I simply don't get it. What did Harrison do that was really so bad? And why won't anyone ever talk about it? This has been going on for twenty years and every time I bring the subject up, I'm told no one wants to discuss it and Juliet gets cross and runs back to Bristol.'

Rosa got to her feet and placed the box of decorations on a nearby footstool. 'Zoe, darling, I don't think Juliet wants to discuss it now, either. You were so young at the time and you don't remember it the way Juliet does. She believes that young man broke her heart, and if that's the way she feels about it, you should try to respect that.'

'Believes?' Juliet raised her brows and her voice. 'It's not a question of belief, Mum. It's a fact. He deceived me, tricked me, lied to me and he did break my heart.'

'Yes, sweetheart. I know that's how you feel. But it wasn't all his fault, you know. As far as the house was concerned, his grandfather was the one to blame, not Harrison.'

'So you've said. Many times. But you didn't hear what he said to me. What he made me feel. What he made me believe. And even after all this time, it hurts. Okay, I may be bearing a grudge, and okay, perhaps twenty years is too long to hate someone I hardly knew. Clearly didn't know, in fact, because nothing he said was true. But it's how I feel and I can't change that. I never want to see that man again. Ever. Okay?' She glared at Zoe as she said the last part.

'Okay.' Zoe glared back. 'But you weren't the only one who was upset by what happened. I may've only been five but I can still remember living at The Grange. I miss my huge room, and the view of Mistletoe Row and the apple orchards beyond. I can still visualise the little painting of the houses and orchards in the distance, beneath the words, Mistletoe room, on my door. I can remember the Christmases there, with every bedroom occupied and guests dancing in the massive hall. The tree, ten times the size of this one, every branch weighed down with decorations. I remember the parties. Ice skating on the lake, and swimming in it in summer. I remember you and Mum crying the day we moved out, and Dad looking so miserable I thought he was going to die. I remember people feeling sorry for us and pointing and whispering. But I also remember that it wasn't all perfect living there. This cottage is far warmer and cosier than that place ever was. Mum and Dad were always busy entertaining, or arguing towards the end, and I barely saw them. Here, I got to spend much more time with them, especially as you ran off to Bristol Uni a couple of years later, and stayed in Bristol to work. You act as if you were the only one who got hurt. It broke Dad's heart to leave there, and Mum's too. Do you ever think about that?'

'Of course I do!' Juliet was stunned by Zoe's remarks. Each time this conversation had developed in the past, it was enough for Juliet to say she didn't want to talk about it, and the subject was quickly changed. This time, Zoe seemed determined. 'I think about it all the time.'

'Sweethearts,' Rosa intervened. 'What's done is done and there's no going back. It was all such a long time ago, but I had no idea you felt that way, Zoe darling. You've never said that before.'

'Because I never get a chance. I was always told to stop and the subject was changed. I soon realised there wasn't any point. I was always shot down. And as you say, Mum, it's old news. I've tried to forget it and put the past behind me. I just wish Juliet could do the same. But she's hit the nail on the head when she said she thinks about it all the time. That's the problem. Losing The Grange is all she ever thinks about. And I don't know exactly why she hates Harrison so much for that. He was only eighteen at the time. It was hardly his fault Dad got into such a dire financial mess. Or that Harrison's grandad bought the place from Dad for a knock-down price, was it?'

'Yes it was!' Juliet leapt up. 'But you wouldn't understand, and I *really* don't want to talk about it.'

'You always say that. But perhaps you should. Mum and Dad got over it. Isn't it time you did the same? Or are you going to hate Harrison Bow for the rest of your life? And please don't say yes to that because that is simply crazy. And for an intelligent, independent woman, crazy is *not* a good look.'

'That's enough!' Rosa said. 'I don't know what's got into you, Zoe to make you bring this whole sorry business up again, but Juliet is only here for a week or two. Let's stop this right now and enjoy the festivities together before she returns to Bristol.'

'Runs away again, you mean. And why are you still telling me off, Mum? Even you think it's a bad thing for her to bear a grudge for so long, yet you still won't tell her she's wrong. But that's her trouble. Juliet is never wrong, is she? It's always someone else's fault as far as she's concerned.'

Juliet gasped. 'That's not true. I don't blame other people. If you knew what happened between me and Harrison, you'd understand how I feel.'

'Then tell me!'

'I can't, Zoe.' Juliet dashed to the door but she stopped and turned as Rosa called after her in strangled tones.

'Juliet, please don't run away. Perhaps your sister's right. Maybe it is time we all sat down and talked about this.'

Juliet's fingers tightened around the edge of the door and tears of frustration and anger pricked at her eyes. 'Do you think I'm wrong, Mum? To not be able to forget what happened, I mean.'

Rosa sighed and nodded slowly as she dropped back down on the chair and reached out her hand to Juliet. She looked so forlorn that it tore at Juliet's heart and even though she didn't want to,' Juliet trudged back over and sat on the arm of the chair, taking the hand her mum offered.

'Yes, sweetheart, I do. But simply because holding grudges only hurts the person doing the holding. I'm not suggesting you're wrong about being hurt by what happened. But Zoe is also right about that.' She stretched out her other hand to Zoe, who took it and smiled lovingly. 'It didn't merely happen to you, darling. It happened to us all. And if anyone should bear a grudge, it should be your father. To be the Bell to lose The Grange was a terrible blow to him, even though it wasn't entirely his fault. The markets collapsing, property prices falling, interest rates rising. They all played a part. Even the house itself. You have no idea how much it cost to keep that place going. And I must take some of the blame, if blame is the right word.' She shook her head and sighed again. 'Yes. Perhaps, on reflection, your father and I did entertain too much. Too many lavish parties and such. But we can't undo what we did. And we have so many wonderful memories.'

'That's true,' Juliet agreed. 'I've got hundreds of memories of living there. But in a way, for me that makes it worse. I miss it, Mum. It was as if I left my heart in that house and I'll never get it back.'

'The house, or your heart?' Zoe said, clearly attempting to lighten the mood.

Juliet pulled a face. 'Both.'

Rosa smiled wanly. 'Zoe is also right about things being better after we moved here. Prior to that, your father and I were arguing, I'll be the first to admit it. When we realised just how bad things were, we tried to cut back on everything. We went from holding lavish parties, drinking champagne and eating the finest food, to shutting up virtually every room in the house, drinking cheap wine and eating beans on toast.' She gave a tiny burst of laughter. 'I'll never forget your father's face when I put that plate in front of him after I had dismissed the cook. But my culinary skills weren't up to much in those days.'

'I liked beans on toast,' Zoe said. 'I still do.'

Rosa nodded. 'So do I, sweetheart.'

'I don't miss the caviar, or the parties. Although I do miss the free-flowing champagne sometimes.' Juliet tried to find some humour in the way she felt. 'It's just the house, not the lifestyle, I miss. And the lake and the grounds. I honestly felt as if I belonged there.'

'Imagine how your father felt.' Rosa gave Juliet a thought-provoking look.

'I do,' Juliet lowered her head. 'I think about that all the time.'

'What's going on in here?' Bernard ambled into the room, a jovial look on his face. 'Oh. I thought the tree would be decorated.' He glanced at each of them in turn and the colour, and laughter, drained from him. 'What's happened now?'

Rosa gave him a loving smile. 'We're having a long overdue talk, darling.'

'A talk?' He tensed visibly. 'Not about The Grange, I hope.'

Rosa nodded. 'Yes. About that and other things from the past. Why don't you join us?'

'Mum!' Juliet protested.

'No, Juliet. Zoe is right. Perhaps it is time we all sat down and talked about it as a family. For the past twenty years we've tried to push it under the carpet. To pretend it didn't happen. To keep a stiff upper lip about the whole business. But all that seems to have done is to keep the pain and hurt with us for all these years. And that, my darlings, is ridiculous. I think we should all say exactly how we feel. Let it all out and maybe then, we can finally heal. I believe your father and I have done that, but you definitely haven't, Juliet, and perhaps, nor has Zoe entirely. We've already started, we may as well continue. Pour us all some sherry, darling.' Rosa nodded to Bernard. 'I think we may need it.'

'Is this wise, darling?' He seemed hesitant. 'Especially after earlier this morning.'

'It's because of this morning that we need to do so.'

'You know best,' he said, walking towards the cocktail cabinet and pouring out four sherries as Juliet and Zoe eyed one another in silence and Rosa squeezed their hands as if for morale support.

'Shall I begin?' Rosa asked, as Bernard handed the drinks around. 'I'll summarise for your father's benefit. It seems our Zoe felt a little sidelined before we moved here, so she's actually glad in many ways that we're living in this cottage. Why she's never mentioned it before is rather concerning. I do wish you had, sweetheart.'

'It's not a huge deal, Mum,' Zoe said. 'I'm not scarred for life or anything. Unlike someone else I could mention.'

'Now, now.' Rosa gave Zoe a reprimanding look, but she leant forward and kissed her on the cheek.

'Sorry,' Zoe said, glancing at Juliet. 'Honestly, Dad. Please don't worry about it. All I meant was that life for me improved when we came here because we were more like a normal family. In the old house, we could go for hours without seeing one another. The place was so big, not to mention the grounds. Here, we can't go five minutes without crossing paths, and I like that. Plus, you and Mum never really had much free time at The Grange. You were always busy running the place, or so it seemed to me.'

'I'm so sorry, sweetheart,' Bernard said. 'I certainly don't miss the upkeep of The Grange. And you're right. Family life definitely improved in many ways when we moved here. I loved the old house. I wish it were still in the family. But I came to terms with losing it a long time ago, and to be completely honest, I don't miss it much at all these days.'

'Neither do I,' said Rosa. 'And I don't miss the company of our so-called friends, either. Our true friends still spend time with us and I firmly believe we have had a better life since we've lived here. Your father and I discussed it during the early years, and we thought you both felt the same. We knew you still felt very strongly about what happened between you and Harrison, Juliet, but what none of us had appreciated, darling, is that you blame Harrison entirely, for us moving out of The Grange.'

'Harrison? For us moving out? Why?' Bernard looked from his wife to Juliet, his brows furrowed and a perplexed look on his face. 'I thought this was all because you felt the boy rejected you, sweetheart, and that you resented him for moving into our former home the minute we moved out. Which I fully understand. As I said, it took me a good few years to not look up at the place and feel a certain resentment towards the family. And I suppose that was why I couldn't talk about it with anyone other than your mother, for many years. Then one day, it no longer seemed important. We're genuinely happier here. I thought you realised that, and felt the same way.'

Juliet shook her head. 'No, Dad. I didn't. I don't.'

'Then why on earth didn't you say something? And you, Zoe?'

Zoe shrugged. 'As I've said. I tried. And now it's no big deal for me. And it was years ago. I only brought it up now because Juliet was in such a tizzy about seeing Harrison this morning. I wanted her to know that the move affected us all in one way or another. That's all. I'm over it.'

'And you, Juliet?' Bernard looked both surprised and concerned. 'Why can't you let go of the past? Why do you blame Harrison for us moving out?'

Juliet took a deep breath and met his eyes. Could she say this after all these years? Could she finally admit this to her family? She closed her eyes as she spoke. She couldn't bear to see the effect her words would have on him. But in the moment of silence that followed, she re-opened them.

'Because it was my fault the Bows got the house from us.'

Rosa and Bernard exchanged astonished looks.

'What?' Rosa was obviously shocked.

'Of course it wasn't,' Bernard said. 'Why would you even think such a thing, sweetheart?'

Neither of them was angry, but they were staring at her in disbelief.

'What on earth makes you think that?' Rosa asked.

She had said it now. She may as well continue. 'Because I met Harrison Bow and I stupidly told him how bad things were for us. And he told his grandad, and his grandad conned you into selling cheaply because he knew how desperately we needed the money. He wouldn't have known that if I hadn't told Harrison and if Harrison hadn't told him. I thought he was kind and handsome and caring. I was miserable and upset because you and Mum had a massive row the night before, which I'd overheard, and in the morning, you shut yourself in your study, and that's how I met him. I went to the lake, as I always did when I was upset or had something on my mind. It was frozen so I was skating, and suddenly, there he was. Just sitting on the bench beside the lake, watching me. I know it sounds crazy, but I fell head over heels in love the minute I saw him, and by the end of that morning, I thought he felt the same. I poured my heart and soul out to him and he stomped on it. He told me he simply had to tell his grandad where he was, and then we would go out on a date. But what he really went to tell him was that the old man could grab a bargain. It was only when I got back that evening after our so-called date, that I realised what I'd done. What he'd done. And that's why I had it out with him in the middle of Mistletoe Row that night.'

No one spoke for a second and then Zoe gave a burst of laughter. 'Good God, sis! You really are crazy. Is that honestly what you think happened?'

'I'm not crazy. It did happen. You were five. You had no idea what was going on.'

'Girls!' Bernard interrupted. He emptied his sherry glass and poured himself another. 'It seems Zoe wasn't the only one who had no idea what was going on.' He sat down on the sofa beside Zoe and looked directly at Juliet. His smile was loving, his voice soft and caring. 'Sweetheart. Why do you think Harrison was at the lake that day? It was because Rufus was in my study and we were discussing a deal. I had already agreed to sell the house to him, in principle. We were meeting to finalise the agreement. Luke was at boarding school at the time, and Rufus, who for some reason had brought Harrison with him, told the lad to go and keep himself busy while we chatted. I don't think Harrison had the slightest idea that his grandfather was about to buy the house. In fact, I know he didn't because even now, I can recall Rufus saying that his grandson would be surprised.'

'What?' Juliet blinked in disbelief. 'But … I don't understand. How? You never mentioned the Bows before that day. I thought Rufus Bow turned up later and made you an offer.'

Bernard nodded. 'He did. In a manner of speaking. I had rejected his first offer. He went away for half an hour or so and when he came back, he actually increased it. So if Harrison did say anything to him, which I very much doubt, the lad actually improved things for us. Is this genuinely what you've believed for all these years? Why on earth didn't you ask about it before?'

Juliet shook her head in horror. 'I couldn't. Don't you see? I thought it was my fault. I couldn't bring myself to tell you and Mum that I'd blabbed our private business to a total stranger and because of that, someone had jumped in and grabbed the house from us.'

Rosa and Bernard looked at one another, shook their heads, and suddenly burst out laughing, as did Zoe.

'What's so funny?' Juliet shot to her feet. 'I've been carrying this guilt and hurt around with me for twenty years and all you three do is laugh?'

'Oh sweetheart,' Rosa said. 'We're so sorry. We're not laughing at you. We're laughing at the complete absurdity of the situation. But you're right. It really isn't a laughing matter. Oh darling.' She got up and hugged Juliet tight, kissing her head and stroking her hair. 'All this time you've felt guilty when there was nothing to feel guilty about. And we've never had a proper discussion about what happened because we were all so keen to keep a stiff upper lip and carry on, as all true-blue Brits do. What awful parents we must be to not have realised.'

'No,' Juliet said, still not really sure what had just happened. 'You're not awful parents. I'm an awful daughter. I simply couldn't own up to being the one who helped to lose us The Grange.'

'But you didn't, sweetheart,' Bernard said, joining his wife in the hug and kiss. 'I was the one who did that. That was down to me, the markets, bad luck and circumstance. Things could have been different, but they weren't. That's just life, darling and we have to accept it. The Bows weren't responsible for our financial difficulties. And Rufus Bow actually offered us a lifeline in many respects. A few more days and the bailiffs would've been pounding on the door. Yes, he got the house for a bargain price, but the plain fact is, no one else wanted it and we couldn't afford to wait for the market to improve. Rufus Bow had wanted The Grange for years and the minute he got wind, no doubt from a mutual friend, that we were having financial difficulties, he contacted me. That was almost a year before the day we did the deal. Neither you nor Harrison had anything to do with it.'

'And let's face it,' Zoe said. 'The man hasn't exactly been happy living there, has he? His favourite grandson walked out. He doesn't have any friends to speak of, and he's as miserable as sin if you ever see him out and about. Which you hardly ever do. Especially not over the last few years.' She got to her feet and sighed. 'Can I join in this hug?'

'Of course you can, sweetheart,' Rosa said, extending her arm to embrace Zoe.

They all hugged in silence for several seconds. Even Cinnamon came and nuzzled her way in, having clearly woken up from her snooze in front of the Aga and wondered where everyone was.

'I'm sorry, sis.' Zoe nudged Juliet in the ribs when they finally eased out of the hug. 'You're right. I did know the Bows would be there this morning. No. Don't get cross again. I was doing it for all the right reasons. Luke and I are friends and we want our families to at least get on, even if they can't be all cosy and warm to one another. Just a hello and a smile will do. Is that too much to ask? It is Christmas, after all. And now that you know Harrison wasn't the evil villain you have thought he was for twenty years, surely we can all be civil to one another?'

'Friends?' Juliet gave her a questioning look. 'What does that mean?'

'What I said. Friends. Oh, and Luke did say he was sorry that he hit your car last night and he'll pay for any damage he may have caused.'

'He did what? That was him?'

'Yes. But he didn't realise it was your car he hit, until today. I may have lied a little at the Christmas tree farm, and told him and Harrison that you were in a bad mood this morning because some idiot hit your wing mirror and drove off. I thought Harrison was going to kill him. But Luke apologised right away and offered to pay. He didn't stop last night because of the weather and because he wanted to get home before Harrison and Kiki arrived.'

'Kiki? The beautiful woman we saw today? Is she … is she Harrison's girlfriend?' Juliet asked as Bernard topped up the sherry glasses.

Zoe shrugged. 'I don't know. I didn't ask. Do you want me to?'

'No I don't! I couldn't care less if he has a girlfriend.'

'Then why did you ask?'

'Girls,' Bernard said, raising his glass in the air. 'Let's have a toast, shall we? Here's to the Bell family, and to us working on our communication skills with one another.' He shook his head and grinned.

'And to our happiest Christmas yet,' Rosa added.

'And to putting the past behind us and making friends,' Zoe said.

'What about you, sweetheart?' Rosa asked, smiling at Juliet. 'What would you like to toast to? Perhaps to a brighter and happier New Year?'

'Ah. About that. I've got something I need to … communicate to you about my future,' Juliet said, with a self-deprecating laugh. 'But let's say cheers and happy Christmas for now, and we'll get to that bit later.'

'Cheers,' they all said, as Cinnamon gave a resounding bark, before curling up on the rug in front of the fire, and letting out the most obnoxious smelling fart.

Chapter Seven

She hadn't changed one bit, simply matured like a fine wine.

Harrison was still reeling from the shock of seeing Juliet, which had affected him far more than he expected. He knew seeing her again might unsettle him a little, but this. This was ridiculous. When he had realised that it was Juliet's car that Luke had hit last night, he wanted to kill his little brother. Which was an insane reaction, even for a Bow. His ancestors were known for doing some pretty crazy things when riled, but on the whole, Harrison was mellow and fairly laid back. At least he thought he was. That woman certainly brought out strong emotions in him.

It had been the same the first time he'd lain eyes on her, twenty years ago. It was a freezing February morning; a grey and cloudy day and his grandfather had taken him to The Grange. Rufus told him he had some business to do with his friend, Bernard Bell and that Harrison should go and entertain himself for an hour and then return to the car. One look at the grounds, and Harrison was in his element.

He walked around, taking in every tree, every nook and cranny of the beautiful gardens, the hedges and paths covered in frost, ornate lead pots filled with winter blooms, life-sized statues standing high on tall, stone plinths, a row of conifers leading to a wood. He would love to live somewhere with grounds like these.

He was a sensitive teenager, according to his grandfather, happy to spend hours outdoors doing nothing in particular, simply enjoying his surroundings, reading a book or sitting in a chair beside a window. Not the usual pastimes for an eighteen-year-old. But he was happy. At least, as happy as you could be when you've just lost your parents within six months of each other. His mum to cancer, his dad to a massive heart attack.

Rufus had taken him and Luke in. They had nowhere else to go. But Luke was away at boarding school and Harrison would soon be off to university, so they wouldn't be spending much time with their grandfather. Prior to his parents' passing, they hadn't seen much of Rufus. There had been some sort of falling out, but Harrison didn't know the details and his parents never talked of it. Neither did Rufus. The old man had been nothing like Harrison's dad though, that much was clear, and Harrison missed his parents every day.

On that particular day, he walked through the woods in the grounds of The Grange and saw the lake. The clouds parted and the sun filtered through the trees until he left the wood and walked out into the open, and felt the full force of it. Not so much the warmth – it was February after all – but the power of the light, and for a moment it had blinded him and he raised his hand to shield his eyes.

Through half-closed lids, he saw her. She looked ethereal as she glided across the ice, small shards flying into the air as her skates cut into it, sparkling in the sunlight. Her hair was the colour of summer, like ripening strawberries. She was dressed from head to toe in white and he wondered if one of the statues had come to life and taken to the ice. He was positively mesmerised, and she was completely unaware that he had walked to the lake and sat on a wooden bench which was covered in frost. He wasn't sure how long he sat and watched her until her skates carved into the ice with a grating sound a short distance away and she stared directly at him.

'Hello,' she said, the look of surprise on her lovely, freckled face replaced by a wondrous smile.

She wasn't exactly beautiful but she took his breath away. It took him a moment or two to reply and then all he said was, 'Hi.'

'What are you doing here?' She moved towards him, her body swaying gracefully as she covered the ice between them.

'Watching you.' He took his hands out of his pockets. Perhaps she would skate right into his arms. But she had stopped a metre or so away from him. 'You should be in the Olympics.'

'Thank you. But I'm not that good.'

'You're perfect. I mean. You look really good to me. On the ice. Skating, I mean. You looked good skating. Not that you don't look good now. You do. Um.' He ran a hand through his hair. 'I'm making a bit of a mess of this. Hi. I'm Harrison. Harrison Bow.' He smiled at her. Could she hear his heart thumping or see the perspiration on his forehead? He didn't reach out his hand; clammy palms were definitely not cool. His mouth was dry. He was having trouble swallowing.

'I'm Juliet. It's lovely to meet you.'

'Juliet? Wow. That's a pretty name.'

'Please don't ask me where my Romeo is. I get that all the time from Mrs D.'

'Mrs D?'

'Oh. Mrs Dobbie. She owns Dobbie's Convenience Store on Mistletoe Row.'

'Mistletoe Row?'

She laughed and it sounded more like angel song. Not that he knew exactly what that sounded like, but her laugh was the most mellifluous sound he'd ever heard.

'You're not from around here, are you?'

'Are you?'

Her brows furrowed a little. 'Are you going to repeat everything I say?'

'Sorry. I mean, do you live near here?'

'Oh. Yes. I live here, actually.'

'The Lady of the Lake?' He raised his brows and performed a dramatic bow. 'It's an honour. May I be your knight in shining armour?'

She laughed again and then hesitated. 'Are you making fun of me?'

'No! Absolutely not.'

She smiled. 'Well okay then.' She gave a delicate curtsy. 'You may.' She skated towards him but one of her blades hit a stone at the edge of the lake and as she fell forwards, he caught her in his arms. 'You are,' she said, looking up into his eyes. 'Thank you for saving me.'

'Anytime, Juliet.'

He wasn't sure how long they stayed like that; his arms around her, her hands on his arms, but he wanted it to be forever.

'Shall we sit?' She pointed hesitantly at the bench.

'I'd like that. Have you lived here all your life? It's so beautiful. I'd love to live in a place like this. Well, to have these grounds. And this lake. You're very lucky.'

She seemed sad, suddenly, and she shook her head. 'It's not all bliss. I think my dad's got money worries. I heard him arguing with my mum.' She looked surprised, as if she hadn't meant to open up to him. 'Sorry. You don't want to hear about my problems.'

'I do, Juliet,' he coaxed, reaching out his hands and taking hers in his. 'I want to hear anything you want to tell me.'

'You'd be bored to tears.'

'No, I wouldn't. Nothing you could say would bore me. Please, Juliet. I'm a good listener.'

And she'd told him quite a lot. She poured out her heart and soul to him and he had listened. So much so that he'd lost all track of time.

'I've got to go,' he said, 'but I wish I didn't have to.'

'So do I,' she replied.

Reluctantly he eased himself away, her hands sliding from his until only their fingers were touching. He curled his fingers tightly round hers. 'Will you go on a date with me? Today? I've just got to go and tell someone where I'll be and then I'll come back.'

She nodded vigorously. 'Yes. Shall I wait here?'

'Yes. I won't be long.'

Without another word, he ran along a different path which he could tell led to the park he and his grandfather had seen as they drove up to the front of the house. He'd never run so fast and when he reached the car, he was out of breath, but his grandfather was nowhere in sight. He could go inside and ask to see him, but that would waste time. Instead, he pulled out the small notepad and pen he always carried around with him and scribbled a note which he pinned under the windscreen wiper. "I'll see you later. I'm spending the day with someone. I've got cash. Will make my own way home. Harrison." He ran back to Juliet as fast as he could.

She was still sitting on the bench, staring at the lake, her skates hanging from her hands resting in her lap. She looked deep in thought. She was now wearing black boots. Black leather boots which came to a point at her knees. She was the sexiest girl he had ever seen and once again, she took his breath away.

'Juliet!' he called out and waved to her.

She seemed startled, but when she turned to face him, sadness drained from her face and was replaced by an excited smile. She looked so beautiful, and even a little vulnerable.

'Harrison! You came back.'

'I said I would. Are you okay?'

She nodded. 'Yes. I'm fine.' Then she sighed as if all the troubles in the world had been lifted from her shoulders. 'That's not true. I'm not. But now that you're back, I feel as if I could be. Does that sound crazy?'

'It doesn't sound crazy at all.'

At some point, he now realised, it must have occurred to him that he should've told her his grandfather was at The Grange with her dad. It also must've occurred to him, deep down, the

71

reason why. But he hadn't said a word. He merely listened. And when, eventually, they had talked of other things, and she had asked what he was doing by the lake that morning, he should've said more than, 'Just admiring the view.' But she hadn't pressed him. She was so caught up in her own troubles that she couldn't really think of anything else, or so it seemed to him.

They had walked, talked, laughed. By the afternoon, they were holding hands as if they were in love. By the evening, they were arm in arm. And when he walked her to the door of The Grange, he had kissed her on the lips.

He could still remember that kiss. Twenty years, and God alone knew how many kisses with other women since, but that kiss was the one that stayed with him. Talk about crazy. He lost his heart to a sixteen-year-old girl that day, and he never got it back.

No. That wasn't exactly true. He had got it back. Later that night, as he stood waiting for a bus to take him to the station in Mistletythe, so that he could get a train home to his grandfather's, she had thrown it back at him, but in tiny little smashed up pieces. She had called him a bloodsucking pariah, and his grandfather too. And she'd told him that she never, ever wanted to see him again for as long as they both lived and that she wished that he were dead.

She had said a few other unpleasant things too, but having only recently lost his parents, being

72

told by the girl he believed could make his future bright and perfect and blissfully happy, that she wished him dead, was really the last thing he had heard.

And later, when he asked his grandfather what happened at the house, and was told that Rufus had been trying to buy the place for a year, but that Bernard Bell had held out until that very day, he felt even more annoyed that Juliet had taken out her frustration on him – an innocent party. Once he'd calmed down, he could see it from her point of view.

'I've got to go back and explain,' he told his grandfather the following day.

'To her? To that Bell girl? To a sixteen-year-old with no money. Don't be ridiculous, Harrison. You have a bright future ahead of you. And so does Luke. Don't throw that away on some silly little girl. You can have any girl you want.'

'She's not a silly little girl, Grandfather. And she's the girl I want. I simply need to make her understand what happened.'

Rufus curled his upper lip and sneered at him. 'The Bows don't go grovelling to the Bells, my boy. They never have and they never will. I did them a favour by paying more than I needed to, to get The Grange. But our family has wanted that place for years and now, we've finally got it. It'll be yours one day, Harrison. Come your thirtieth birthday, you'll inherit the place. We can be the grand family we always should've been. You need to marry someone who can add to our wealth, not some girl who'll waste it like her foolish father has.'

Harrison laughed mirthlessly. 'I don't want to be a *grand* family. And when I marry, it'll be for love, not money. This is 1998, Grandfather, not 1798. Stuff like that doesn't matter these days. It hasn't done for decades.'

'It matters to families like ours, my boy. And believe me, it matters to the Bells, too. That girl would like nothing more than to get the house back, and what better way than to make the man who'll eventually own it, fall head over heels in love with her. Did it even occur to you that she knew exactly who you were? Good God, boy. Have you no sense whatsoever? Apart from the fact you only met the girl yesterday, can't you see what she's doing?'

Harrison was thrown off balance for a second. 'No. She hadn't a clue who I was. That's why she was so mad with me. I'm going to see her, Grandfather, whether you like it or not. And, yes, I've only known her for one day, but Mum once told me that when you meet your soulmate, you know. You feel it in every part of you. I felt it when I saw Juliet. And I believe she felt it too.'

Rufus thumped his fist on the desk and leapt to his feet. 'Your mother was an idiot, Harrison. She lived in the land of fairy tales. My son should never have married her, but like you, he wouldn't listen. Well, there was nothing I could do to stop him throwing his life away over a silly girl. But there is something I can do to stop you from making the same mistake.'

Harrison clenched his fists and glowered. 'Don't ever call my mother that again. She and Dad were deeply in love until the day they died. They were happy, unlike you. I'm sorry to have to break this to you, Grandfather, but just like with my dad, there's nothing you can say or do to make me change my mind.'

'Oh, isn't there?' Rufus said as Harrison turned to leave the room. 'Do you want to ruin your little brother's life too? Because that's exactly what you'll do if you go back to that girl. Today, or any day from now. Who do you think's paying for him to be at that posh school of his, eh? Who provides him – and you for that matter – with a roof over your heads? Stay away from that girl or believe me, things will change around here. And not for the better as far as Luke's concerned. I hope I have made myself clear.'

Harrison sucked in a breath but he didn't turn around.

'Even if it means I'll hate you for the rest of your life?'

Rufus gave a snort of derision. 'You won't hate me. I'm blood. But yes. Even then.'

Harrison had no choice. He could never do anything to jeopardize Luke's future; the ten-year-old had gone through enough.

So they had moved into The Grange and Harrison spent the little time he was there, walking around the grounds, or locked in his room with a book and when he'd left a few weeks later to do some volunteer work abroad before starting university, he vowed he would never set foot inside The Grange again, nor drive along Mistletoe Row, the scene of one of the unhappiest times of his life.

And until last night, he hadn't.

Chapter Eight

Juliet needed some fresh air. The sun was still shining and it was so much warmer, yet Cinnamon was still curled up in front of the Aga where she'd gone as soon as the family went into the kitchen for lunch.

'I'm taking Cinnamon for a walk. Do you want anything from the shop, Mum?'

'No thank you, sweetheart. You got everything we needed yesterday.'

'D'you want some company?' Zoe looked up from the magazine she was reading and smiled.

'That'd be nice.'

They grabbed their coats from the hall and walked out into the sunshine on Mistletoe Row, both of them turning to look up at The Grange. They glanced at one another and laughed.

'God. We're so predictable,' Zoe said. 'I knew you'd do that, and then I go and do the same.' She shook her head and sighed. 'So much for me being over it.'

'I'm not sure any of us will ever be over leaving there. It was a part of who we are. It's been in the Bell family for centuries. Not that exact house, of course, but parts of it. Do you remember the old photos and paintings hanging on the walls in the Gallery? The ones of the house throughout the centuries, not the paintings of our ancestors, I mean.'

Zoe shook her head. 'Not really. But I've seen all the photos Mum and Dad took before we left. It must've felt awful for Dad, leaving all those paintings behind. It's a bit like us moving out of the cottage now and leaving our photo albums and digital photos for the new owners. It's weird, isn't it?'

'Not as weird as it must be for the Bows to have to walk around and look at them. Are they still there, I wonder? I mean, perhaps that old git sold them all. Or put them in storage. Or gave them away.'

'Don't get upset. Your voice was rising with each sentence. They're all still there.'

Juliet stopped and looked Zoe in the eyes. 'Are they? How do you know? Oh. I suppose Daphne told Mum, didn't she? They're quite friendly, aren't they?'

'Yes. She pops in for tea sometimes. She's invited Mum up to The Grange, but of course Mum says no. Not because it would upset her, although I think it might in spite of everything they said today. She doesn't go because if old Bow found out she was there, he'd probably sack Daphne on the spot.' Zoe bit her lower lip. 'But I know nothing's changed at the house, well nothing much anyway because Luke told me it hadn't. He said if I walked back in there tomorrow, it would be as if I'd never left. He's said I could go, if I want, but I've always said no because if it is still the same, that would make it feel weird and it'd bring it all back again.'

Juliet sighed. 'I'd love to see the place again. Even if it did break my heart to do so.'

'I thought your heart was still broken from all those years ago? Sorry. Bad joke.'

'It is. Or it was. Now I don't know what to feel. What Mum and Dad said today was a real surprise. I had no idea Dad had been thinking of selling for over a year, did you? Oh, sorry, of course you didn't. You were five. The only thing that interested you were your Barbie dolls.'

'Yeah. I had a big crush on Ken. I don't think I've ever got over it.'

'Oh very funny.' Juliet gave Zoe a playful shove. 'Seriously though. What Mum and Dad said does sort of change things a bit. All these years I've been blaming myself – and Harrison, and it turns out it was nothing to do with either of us.'

'Yep. And just think. All of this heartache could so easily have been resolved, if only we were the sort of family who told each other things.

And gave other people a chance to explain. Or even to say hello, before jumping into a car and slouching behind the seats like a child.'

Juliet tutted. 'I suppose that's a dig at me for this morning, isn't it? But come on. In twenty years, has he ever tried to explain? Or even tried to write to me? Or, since the popularity of social media, tried to find me on there and send me a friend request? Or anything, in fact?'

Zoe tipped her head from side to side. She often did that when she was thinking and Juliet smiled at her, now really glad to be home and with her family.

'No. You're right. He's never made the slightest effort to explain. Or to try to be friends. But have you ever wondered if there might be a reason for that? Apart from the obvious one of you snapping his head off the moment he came near, of course.'

'Like what?'

'I don't know. I'm just saying. You've said you thought you and he both fell in love at first sight but that you then discovered he was a liar, et cetera and you told him to get lost, and to never darken your door again. Or something along those lines.'

'Yeah. So?'

'So. Maybe that just proves he's the perfect gentleman. That he's noble and kind. Or something. What I'm saying is, perhaps he was simply doing what you told him to. What he thought you wanted. And that's why he's stayed away. Perhaps the guy's too bloody nice and moral and stuff like that. Even though his own heart is broken, he'll die before he hurts you again. You know, like a real knight in shining armour. Perhaps he's your Romeo, and he'll die for you.'

'I think you need to reread your Shakespeare, Zoe. That's not quite the plot. Romeo drinks the poison because he thinks Juliet's dead and he can't live without her. Then she wakes up, sees he's dead, goes on a bit about how unfair life is and all that stuff, then stabs herself because she can't bear life without him either.'

'Whatever. Hmm. Shakespeare in three sentences. I like it. Perhaps we should put on a Christmas play. The Bells do Shakespeare. What do you think?'

'That you need to get a life.'

'Hey. Look who's talking.' Zoe bent down and picked up a handful of snow.

Juliet pointed a finger at her. 'Put that down right now. I mean it, Zoe. Don't even think about it. Oww!'

The snowball hit Juliet in the centre of her chest and Zoe roared with laughter, while Cinnamon barked and jumped around in little circles, kicking up showers of melting snow. Almost as if the dog was joining Zoe in a victory dance.

'Right. You asked for it.'

Juliet let go of Cinnamon's lead and shovelled up snow with her gloved hands. Zoe hurriedly did the same and snowballs careered back and forth for several minutes, some of which hit Cinnamon, who whimpered, ran away and then came pelting towards them, knocking each of them flying, in turn. Juliet and Zoe lay on the snow, both curled up with laughter.

'I think Cinnamon won.' A man's voice said.

Juliet sat bolt upright and looked directly up at Luke Bow, standing just a few metres away. Panic set in immediately and her eyes searched frantically for his brother. Thankfully, Harrison was nowhere to be seen.

'Cinnamon cheated,' Zoe said, sitting upright too and stretching out her hands towards Luke.

To Juliet's surprise, he rushed to Zoe to help her up, before offering a hand to Juliet. She hesitated for a second but saw the look on Zoe's face, and gave in.

'Thank you, Luke,' she said, brushing snow from her coat and grabbing Cinnamon's lead as it dragged by her feet.

'Anytime,' he replied. 'Er. And maybe now would be a good time to tell you how sorry I am about your wing mirror. Did Zoe tell you I'll happily pay for any damage?'

Juliet nodded. 'She did. Thank you. But to be honest, there isn't much. Just a scratch or two, and considering how many other scratches there are on my car, one or two more won't make much difference. I was worried the glass might be broken, but thankfully it wasn't.'

'Harrison gave me a real bollocking last night when I told him I'd hit someone's wing mirror, and when he found out this morning that it was your car – Whew! I thought I was dead meat. Listen. If you don't want me to pay for it, what else can I do to make amends?'

Juliet shook her head. 'There's no need.'

Luke laughed. 'Oh yes there is. Big bro says so.'

'You could let her skate on the lake,' Zoe said.

Luke glanced from Juliet to Zoe and back again. 'The lake? The one in the grounds?'

Zoe tutted. 'No. The one in Hyde Park. Of course the one in the grounds, genius.'

'Okay. No need to get all high and mighty. Juliet can skate on the lake whenever she wants. So can you.'

'Thanks. But I'm not a skater.'

'And thank you,' Juliet added. 'But I'm not sure your grandad would approve.'

'Who cares what he thinks? Besides, Harrison as good as runs the place these days, albeit from afar. And he'd be more than happy for you to do anything you want on the lake. Hey, Zoe. I can teach you if you want. I'm not very good though.'

'If I wanted someone to teach me, I'd ask Juliet. She's brilliant.'

Juliet laughed. 'Maybe when I was younger, but I haven't skated much since … well, not for years. I'd probably spend more time on my backside than my blades.'

'Now's the time to find out,' Zoe said. 'What about tomorrow morning? Around ten, let's say.'

Luke shrugged. 'Sounds good to me. Tell you what. Why don't we all go?'

'No!' Zoe shot a look at Juliet before smiling at Luke. 'I think Juliet would prefer to be alone, wouldn't you?'

Juliet looked from her sister to Luke and back again. She longed to skate on the lake once more. That was one of the things she had missed. She'd skated on rinks in Bristol once or twice but it wasn't the same. Nowhere near. There was something about the lake at The Grange that was magical. It was large, for one thing. And it was sheltered by trees on two sides – the wood, and a small apple orchard, which would be filled with mistletoe at this time of year, just like the orchards either side of Mistletythe Lane. To feel the cold wind in her hair as she skated on the lake, after all these years, would be a dream come true.

'If I were to take you up on the offer then yes, I'd rather skate alone. At least, for a little while.'

'Fine by me. I'll tell Daphne you'll be there. Just in case she looks out and thinks someone is trespassing. Not that you would be. But Grandfather is hot on that sort of thing and if

Daphne knows you're there, it'll mean she can keep him at bay.'

'Oh. I don't want to cause any trouble.'

Luke smiled warmly. 'You won't be, I assure you. Far from it.'

'And Harrison?'

'What about him?'

'He may very well object.'

'Nah. Besides, I won't tell him. He's got Kiki with him so they'll be pretty busy anyway.'

That was not what Juliet wanted to hear. She could easily imagine how busy the man would be. And who could blame him? Kiki was the most beautiful woman in the world, after all. With a figure to match, from the brief look Juliet got of her that morning.

Not that she was jealous or anything.

Damn the woman.

Chapter Nine

He may as well accept it. Even after twenty years it was clear Juliet was never going to acknowledge that she might have been wrong about him. Or at the very least, may have judged him harshly for any part he may have inadvertently played in his grandfather's purchase of The Grange.

When Luke had asked him to come and spend Christmas and to try to put the past behind them, a tiny part of him had hoped he might bump into Juliet and that she would smile that smile of hers; the one he still remembered after all these years. That she would say hello, ask how he was, and tell him she was sorry for the way things turned out between them. He'd invite her for a coffee, or perhaps a glass of wine. Not dinner. It would be too soon for dinner. He didn't want to rush things this time. She'd say yes, of course, and they'd spend a convivial hour or so catching up with one another's lives. He knew she hadn't married. Luke had kept him informed in passing and once Daphne moved in and became friends with Juliet's mum, he gleaned a few more details. He would suggest a walk, and somehow, he'd work it so that they ended up at the lake, possibly as the sun was setting. Once there, they'd sit on the bench, as they had twenty years ago, and it would all come flooding back. The way they looked at one another, the way they felt.

Or did that kind of thing only happen in romance novels and films?

It certainly hadn't gone that way in real life. She hadn't looked into his eyes that morning and rushed into his arms. She hadn't even smiled. If looks could kill, he'd be dead and buried, six feet under. She had taken one look at him and fled like a gazelle with a lion at her heels. She'd shut herself in her dad's car and skulked behind the seats as if he were one of the walking dead and she had to hide from him at all costs.

So probably no point in calling round and asking her out for coffee then?

God, what an absolute loser he was. He'd spent twenty years as good as pining for his so-called lost love and all she does is ignore him. Perhaps it was time he got the message. Juliet Bell would never admit that she was wrong. And she'd never give him the time of day, let alone go on a date.

'Yoo-hoo. Harrison. Luke says we're going to the pub.' Kiki's sultry tones wafted along the hall from the doorway of the Dawn room and Harrison smirked.

He'd foolishly asked Daphne to move Kiki from the Rose room last night when he'd gone downstairs for dinner.

'Certainly, Harrison,' Daphne had said, looking a little bewildered. 'I assumed you would want your assistant to be near to you, but yes, I'll move her to a room at the other end of the hall. Leave it with me. I'll have the Dawn room ready before you've finished dinner.'

And she had.

'Why am I moving rooms?' Kiki asked when he went back upstairs and told her he needed her to repack anything she had unpacked so that he or Luke could take her luggage to another room.

'Because the Rose room isn't the room you should be in. I want you to be able to see the sun rise, and you can do that from the Dawn room.'

'But I'm not a morning person.'

'Then now's as good a time as any to adjust. Believe me, we'll both be much happier if you're in Dawn. It's a lovely room. And you've always said pink is so not your colour.'

'Wow. I'm impressed that you remembered. Okay, Harrison. If it'll make you happy.'

She had baulked when she saw it was at the other end of the hall though.

'I'm a restless sleeper, Kiki. I get up and wander around a lot. This way, if I'm constantly opening and closing my door, you won't be disturbed.'

'Aw, Harrison. You're the best boss in the world, and such a good friend. Don't let anyone tell you otherwise. But if you feel like wandering in the direction of my room, I won't be that upset.'

'Good to know. Thanks,' he said.

Well, perhaps that was exactly what he should do. Kiki was gorgeous after all, with a fantastic body and legs that went on forever. Would it be so bad to get entangled in those legs? She was fun to be with. She laughed at his pathetic jokes. She was always ready and willing to do anything for him. She even gave up going skiing in Aspen with her brother to come and spend Christmas at a dingy old house with him, his brother and their miserable old grandfather. Did it get any better than that? What on earth was he waiting for?

For Juliet?

Forget it. Forget her. Get over it. Twenty years is far too long to hold on to a memory and a vision of what might have been. That ship had sailed, crashed on the rocks and sunk to the bottom of the ocean.

Luke had asked him to come for Christmas and to put the past behind him. Well, okay. That was exactly what he was going to do. And as they were going to the pub for the evening, tonight would be a good time to start.

'You were very quiet on the way here?' Kiki said, as they got out of Luke's car in the small car park at the rear of The Mistletoe pub.

'Was I? Sorry.' Harrison smiled at her as she linked her arm through his.

'You don't mind, do you?' She looked him directly in the eye. 'It's so icy here and I don't want to slip.'

'I don't mind at all. There'll be ice everywhere so watch your step. The warmth of today melted a lot of the snow and now the temperature's dropped again, it's turned to ice.'

'Thanks for stating the obvious,' Luke said, grinning at Harrison. 'Is this really going to be only the second time you've been in this pub? Didn't you come here during the summer before you left for uni?'

Harrison shook his head. 'No. I kept myself to myself and stayed at the house and then went off to do volunteer work cleaning up a reef or two in the Pacific. It was a hard job, but someone had to do it.' He grinned at Luke. 'And there's a fully-stocked bar at the house, so while I was here, I didn't need to venture out. Besides, I didn't feel much like company at the time.'

'Why not?' Kiki asked, her silky, mahogany hair shimmering in the glow from the myriad fairy lights hanging from every available centimetre of roof, windows and doors of the pub.

'I was eighteen and a very moody teenager but unlike most, I was more into books and nature than I was alcohol and going out. And nothing much has changed in twenty years.'

'Except you're not eighteen anymore,' Luke teased.

'Yeah. Thanks for reminding me. And after we moved into The Grange, coming here once was more than enough. This place hasn't changed from the outside in all that time. Do the Dobbie's still own it?'

'Yep. Kevin and his second wife, Paula. He was still married to the first one the last time you came here. Were you friends with Dan? He's around your age.'

'No. Never met him.'

'Who's Dan?' Kiki asked.

Luke opened the rear door to the pub and held it for her and Harrison. 'He's Kevin's son. He always comes to stay at some stage over the Christmas holidays, so you'll get to meet him. I don't really know him, but we've seen each other around and we say hello and stuff. He lives with his mum in Norway, or somewhere cold like that.'

Harrison raised his brows. 'Let's hope there's not a pub quiz.' He slapped Luke playfully on his arm. 'Somewhere cold like that. God, Luke, remind me never to ask you for tips on holiday destinations.'

'You never ask me for tips on anything, so a reminder won't be necessary.'

. Harrison looked at his brother. Was that a mild gripe? Luke's way of saying that Harrison didn't give him enough of his attention? Or discuss things with him? Was Luke feeling sidelined? Left out of Harrison's life? God. Everything he had done had been for Luke's benefit. Well, nearly everything. He had been determined to be successful, and wealthy in his own right, so that neither he nor Luke would ever again have to depend on their grandfather, or look to the old man for support. And Harrison had definitely succeeded in that. But by the time he had, Luke was settled and happy with the way things were. He actually liked living at The Grange. He took friends there during school holidays. On the one occasion Harrison had suggested Luke should live with him, Luke had turned him down.

'I can't leave the old man on his own, bro,' he had said. 'He's always going on about how heart-breaking it was when you walked out on him. It'd kill him if I did the same.'

There was no point in explaining what had really happened. Luke had a soft spot for the old man, and thankfully it seemed, the old man felt the same about Luke. Harrison couldn't ruin that relationship for his brother. It simply wouldn't be fair to him. And Luke didn't need to know the threat the old man had made. Telling him might make Harrison feel happier but it wouldn't do anything for Luke.

But surely Luke knew that he was the most important person in Harrison's life? That Harrison thought the world of him. That the only reason he was here right now was because Luke had wanted him to come?

Apparently not, if that remark was anything to go by. Harrison clearly had some bridges to build. And he had better start that without delay.

'What do you recommend, Luke?' Harrison asked as they strolled towards the bar. 'Is there a local beer?'

Luke shrugged. 'I'm having a G&T. I don't drink beer much. Kevin can suggest one though.'

Of course Luke didn't drink beer. Harrison knew that. Luke always drank G&T when they were together. This wasn't getting off to a good start.

Harrison smiled. 'Great tip. I'll ask Kevin. Kiki? White wine?'

'No thanks. I think I'll have a Bailey's. A double, please.'

Could he get anything right tonight? Why had the pub gone suddenly quiet? He glanced around and noticed several of the customers were staring at him. He should've expected it, really. News of his reappearance must have spread the length and breadth of Mistletoe Row by now. He was well aware that people still talked about the Bows buying The Grange from the Bells, even after all this time. Well, conning the Bells into selling it cheaply and kicking them out onto the street with just the clothes on their backs, was closer to the story at the time. And that probably hadn't changed in twenty years either.

Harrison smiled at the portly, late-middle-aged man behind the bar. 'Good evening. Kevin, is it? I'm Harrison, Luke's brother.'

'I know who you are,' came the reply, without the slightest hint of a smile.

'Excellent. We'd like a double Bailey's with ice, please. One G&T. Might as well make that a double too. And a pint of whichever beer you recommend. Thanks. Oh, and whatever you'd like for yourself and your good wife, and a round of what everyone else is drinking, as it's Christmas and my *happy* homecoming.'

For a split second, no one reacted; his smile was met with complete silence, and then a bubbly-looking woman, who was obviously Paula Dobbie, flashed him a smile that actually looked genuine. There was laughter in her voice as she eyed him up and down.

'So you're Harrison Bow, are you? I'm Paula. Kevin's wife. Let me get a good look at you. I wasn't here the last time you were, but I've heard the stories, same as everyone else, and I have to say, you don't look half as bad as they all said you would. I was expecting the devil himself. Get the man his drinks, Kevin.' She nudged her husband's arm none too gently, and shook a finger with a long, red-painted nail at the crowded room. 'And the least you lot can do is say thank you. No one else comes in here and offers to buy you all a drink, do they? It's Christmas. Goodwill to all men and all the rest of it. I'll have a Bailey's too, thanks very much, Harrison.'

The room burst into a cacophony of voices. Thanks, pats on the back, and friendly greetings abounded.

Even Kevin smiled as he poured Harrison a pint. 'This here's Mistletoe Magic. It's from a small, independent brewery in Mistletythe. Give it a try and see what you think.'

'Thanks. It's a good colour. I'm sure it'll taste good too.'

Paula winked at him as she poured herself a Bailey's and he beamed at her. 'Thank you, Paula.'

'Don't mention it, love. This is going to cost you a pretty penny.'

'It's worth it, Paula.' He took a drink of the beer Kevin put in front of him. 'That is good, Kevin. I'll definitely have this again.'

'And I'll have a pint myself. Thank you kindly, Harrison.'

Harrison nodded. 'You're welcome.'

He hadn't really wanted to come to the pub this evening. He knew his name was probably still mud around here. But Luke asked him to, so he had, and now he was glad of it. Paula was lovely and so was Kevin. And the rest of the crowd were okay too. He simply had to make an effort to get to know them. It would be great to be able to come to the local pub while he was here. He was happy in his own company but everyone liked to socialise and he was no exception.

'Well,' Luke said, grinning as Harrison handed him his G&T and they walked towards a vacant table. 'It seems you've made some new friends.'

Kiki pulled a face and took a sip of her Bailey's. 'Money can buy you anything, Luke. Haven't you realised that by now?'

Chapter Ten

It was the perfect weather for ice skating when Juliet threw open the curtains on Tuesday morning. Crisp and clear. There was a slight frost on the ground but the sun was already turning it to vapour and little smoke-like wisps rose up from the pavement and dissipated into the cool, morning air.

She showered, threw on a pair of black ski pants, a black jumper with a flashing green and red Christmas tree emblazoned on the front, and black, knee-high boots. A memory flashed into her mind; she had worn similar boots all those years ago when she had sat on the bench waiting for Harrison. She quickly dismissed the image, brushed her lashes with a dab of mascara, covered her lips with winter cherry lip balm and dashed downstairs.

Her ice skates hung over the back of one of the kitchen chairs, exactly where she had left them last night. Who knew that being made redundant and having to move home would have an upside? If not for that, she would have left her ice skates in her flat in Bristol. Other than the lake at The Grange, there was nowhere within a thirty-mile radius of Mistletythe to skate, and she would not, for one minute, have expected to be able to skate at the lake, in the normal course of events. But nothing about this festive season so far was normal. The redundancy, moving home, the heart-to-heart with her family, and Luke Bow offering to let her skate on the lake; definitely not the usual Christmastime.

'Morning all,' she chirped, as she sat at the kitchen table for breakfast and everyone returned her cheery greeting.

'You're full of the joys of Christmas,' Rosa said, kissing the top of Juliet's head as she stood behind her and leant over to pour her a cup of coffee.

'It's a beautiful day, and I'm going skating on the lake. There's a lot to be joyful about. What are your plans for the day? I'll be back in time for lunch.'

'I plan to do as little as possible,' Bernard said, a huge grin on his face as he scooped up a spoonful of porridge. 'There's a new murder mystery I'm longing to read.'

Rosa pulled a face. 'Perhaps I'll do the same, darling. Oh wait. Someone needs to clean the kitchen, bake some more mince pies, write the list for the big Christmas shop, do the washing. Need I continue?' She blew her husband a kiss.

'No, no. Message received and understood. Tell me what you need me to do, my darling, and I'll happily do it.'

'I'll give you a list,' she replied, with a loving smile.

'I can do some of that when I get back,' Juliet said. 'And Zoe will help, won't you?'

'Huh?' Zoe glanced up from the magazine she was reading. 'Won't I what?' She glanced at each of them in turn.

'Help around the house, sweetheart,' Rosa said, refilling Zoe's coffee cup.

'Yeah. Of course I will. After I've taken Cinnamon for her walk. Just tell me what you want me to do, and consider it done.'

Rosa smiled. 'Goodness me. Father Christmas will be proud of you all. What a band of merry little helpers you all are this morning. We must have family heart-to-hearts more often if this is the result.' She walked back around the table and rested a hand on Juliet's shoulder. 'What would you like for breakfast, sweetheart?'

'Just toast for me. But I'll get it, Mum. You sit down before your porridge gets cold.' Juliet got up and walked over to the toaster. 'Anyone else for toast?'

'Yes please,' each of them said in unison, and Cinnamon barked and raised her head.

Juliet laughed. 'Even the dog wants some. I shouldn't have asked. Thank heavens it's an eight-slice toaster.'

'Are you driving to the house?' Rosa asked.

Juliet tensed slightly. 'No. I thought I'd walk across the park, through the apple orchard and sneak in the back gate. Luke said it would be unlocked when I mentioned it yesterday. I really don't want to come face-to-face with old Bow.'

'Harrison?' Zoe said, grinning.

Juliet grinned back. 'Not that one. The other one.'

'I don't think there's much chance of that,' Rosa said. 'From what Daphne tells me, Rufus rarely goes further than his bedroom, his study, or the dining room. It's a good thing he can't see the lake from any of those rooms.'

'Yeah. He'd probably have an apoplexy if he saw me skating on his lake. He'd set the dogs on me.'

'I didn't know they had dogs,' Bernard said.

Rosa shook her head. 'They don't, darling. It's a figure of speech.'

'They should have dogs.' There was a thoughtful look on Bernard's face. 'A house isn't a home without dogs.'

'Luke likes dogs,' Zoe said.

'So does Harrison.' Juliet bit her lip. 'I mean, so *did* Harrison. At least he said he did. But then he said a lot of things. Sorry. Not going there again. Okay. So I'll be back around twelve-ish.

We'll have lunch and then do stuff around the house. Yes?'

'Sounds like a plan,' Rosa said.

'It's always good to have a plan,' replied Bernard.

'Absolutely,' agreed Juliet.

Zoe grinned mischievously. 'I'm glad you all think that.'

'Oh?' Rosa gave her a curious look. 'Don't you then, sweetheart?'

'I definitely do. In fact, I have a couple of plans of my own. But they're top secret and on a strictly need-to-know basis.' She beamed at each of them. 'And for now, none of you need to know.'

'I hope your plan includes getting me a lovely Christmas present,' Juliet said, hastily eating her toast and draining the last dregs from her coffee cup.

'Oh it does, sis. And you have no idea how lovely.'

Juliet grinned at Zoe and rose to leave. 'Right. I'm out of here. See you all later. Have fun.'

'You too,' everyone replied.

Juliet grabbed her skates, almost falling over Cinnamon, who was munching a slice of buttered toast, retrieved her thick, black jacket from the coat hook and dashed out the front door onto an icy, Mistletoe Row. She nearly landed on her backside as her feet slipped beneath her, but she managed to grab the door handle and steady herself.

'That's twice I've almost fallen over,' she said out loud. 'And everything comes in threes.' She shook her head and sighed.

Glancing at her watch, she saw it was ten-to-ten and yet there wasn't a car in sight. No people, either. But it was such a lovely day. She took a deep breath of the cool, crisp morning air and then walked gingerly over the road to the park, where the ground was still covered in snow. She ran across the snow-covered grass, through the apple orchard and made her way to the back gate of the grounds and gardens of The Grange. The gate was unlocked, as Luke said it would be, but she hesitated before she pushed it open. This would be the first time in twenty years that she had set foot on this hallowed ground and she needed a moment to let it sink in.

Only a brief moment though. Her excitement got the better of her. She shoved the ornate, wrought iron gate open and quickly closed it behind her. The path was slippery but she didn't care. She ran, slipping and sliding as she went, to the lake, stopping the second she saw it.

Its beauty took her breath away. It hadn't changed one bit. Even the bench looked the same, but perhaps a little older and more weathered. She raced towards it.

'Hello bench,' she said, laughing heartily at her foolishness and then she sat, almost reverently, and sighed. Dropping her skates beside her, she stared ahead at the lake. 'Hello lake. You have no idea how much I've missed you.'

If it could talk, she was sure it would say the same.

It was several minutes before she looked away and she took a long, deep breath as she slipped off her boots and put on her skates.

She got up and stepped onto the ice and it was as if something magical shot through her entire body, from her feet to her head. She closed her eyes, stretched out her arms, gracefully shaping her fingers like those of an ice dancer, and pushed away with her left foot. She skated in circles of eight, moving her hands behind her and clasping her fingers as she retraced her glide path backwards. She lowered her body, bending one knee and stretching her other leg out in front of her.

Raising herself upright, she leapt into the air, stretching her legs wide apart and reaching forward to touch her toes, landing gracefully as she skated forward into a spin. That was followed by more jumps; a triple axel, a double Lutz. She was in her element. Her skin was glowing in the warmth of the sun, her blood was racing through her veins, her muscles flexed and toned. She didn't want to stop.

Skating faster, she made a circuit of the lake, and another. More jumps, more spins. She could stay there all day. Fleetingly, she saw a figure out of the corner of her eye. Had Luke come down to greet her? She carved her blades into the ice and skated into an area where she was blinded by the sun. She closed her eyes against the glare but as she moved forward she heard the crack and felt her blade catch as she came to an abrupt stop. She glanced down as lines, like lots of little blood vessels, fanned out from where she stood. Her eyes shot towards the figure and only now did she see who it was.

'Harrison!' she shrieked as the ice cracked open and she fell into the freezing waters of the lake.

Chapter Eleven

Harrison thought his imagination was running wild. Had his mind gone back twenty years and made his eyes project an image of something he had once seen? Although now she was dressed in black; twenty years ago, she was dressed in white.

But as he walked towards the lake, the sun filtering through the trees and warming his face, he was sure of one thing. That was definitely Juliet skating on the lake.

What was she doing there? How did she get in? His grandfather disliked trespassers so the back gate to the grounds would definitely have been locked – unless someone had opened it for her. Perhaps she still had a key. Perhaps the old man hadn't changed the locks.

Did it really matter? She was there. He wasn't imagining it. He could hear the swish of her blades as she swept across the ice. The gentle thud as she landed gracefully after each jump. Yes. She was definitely real, not a figment of his imagination. She was there and so was he.

Should he stay and watch? Should he go and sit on the bench as he had all those years ago? Should he turn and walk away before she spotted him, and turned and ran away herself?

And then he heard it. The unmistakable crack. The rest of the world seemed silent as his ears focused on the terrifying sound. The ice was breaking, and it was breaking beneath Juliet.

From a distance, their eyes met, the fear in hers matching the panic in his. He heard her call his name, at least he thought she did, and then she dropped like a stone before him, her outstretched fingers the last thing he saw as she disappeared beneath the ice.

He was already running although he hadn't realised that until he was slipping and sliding towards the gaping hole. There wasn't time to think and as foolish as it was, he jumped in after her.

All around was dark at first and then he saw the shafts of sunlight dappled through the water. He twisted and turned, his eyes darting here, there and everywhere until he saw her. He dived down, grabbed her hand and pulled her towards him, searching for the light once he was sure of his grip on her. He had never believed in miracles, but he believed in them now. A wide beam of light was a mere metre or so away and he swam towards it as fast as possible, gasping for air as he broke through the surface water.

But he didn't have time to stop. He had to get her out, before the weight of the freezing water in their clothes dragged them down again. He put his hands on Juliet's waist and with Herculean effort, he pushed her out of the water onto a shelf of ice. The task pushed him below the surface but he found his way back and hauled himself onto the ice beside her.

He had no time to waste but the ice here was also at risk of breaking, so in a prostrate position he dragged Juliet and himself towards firmer ice. Once there, he got to his feet, swept her limp body up into his arms and rushed to the safety of the bank.

Chapter Twelve

Either she was dreaming, or she was dead. There was no other way she could possibly be back in her former bedroom at The Grange.

Juliet blinked several times before reaching out to touch the bedside table. It certainly felt real. But then again, didn't everything in a dream feel real? When she dreamt of falling, it always felt as if she actually was. And more than once she had woken, crying, from a dream.

'Juliet?' The voice certainly sounded real. And it was Harrison's. Clearer and closer than it had been when she'd heard it at the Christmas tree farm on Monday. It sounded a little deeper than it had, and there was a fearful quality to it. But it was definitely his. 'Juliet? Can you hear me?'

'Yes, Harrison. I can hear you. But my head hurts. Am I dreaming? Or am I dead?'

A sigh of relief; a gurgle of laughter; a touch of a hand.

'Neither, Juliet. But you came pretty close to the latter.'

Memory streamed in on her and she tried to sit up, but the effort was too much. She fell back onto her pillows and sunk into the softness as if her head rested on a cloud. But it was still hurting. Why did her head hurt? Had she hit it? No. But the last thing she could remember was dropping through the ice like a bullet and being surrounded by darkness and cold.

'What happened?'

Daphne's voice now. 'You fell through the ice, dear.'

'That much I remember.' Juliet tried to focus as Daphne busied herself adjusting the bedding and adding more blankets.

'Are you warm enough?' Daphne asked.

'Yes thanks. Very. But what happened after I fell through the ice?'

'Harrison saved you, dear. He had to give you the kiss of life. Thank heavens he was there, otherwise God alone knows where you'd be right now.'

'At the bottom of the lake, I expect. Wait. What? He gave me the …' She turned startled eyes towards where his voice had come from and saw he sat by her bed. 'You gave me the kiss of life? You saved me?'

'Just in the right place at the right time.' He gave a nonchalant shrug.

'But … You jumped into the lake and pulled me out? Just like that?'

He smiled. 'Not, just like that. But yeah. What else could I do?'

'You could've let me drown. No one would blame you. No one would've known. You could've walked away and pretended you weren't even there.'

His face grew serious and he frowned as his voice sounded cross. 'Why in God's name would I do that?'

Juliet lowered her lashes and looked away. 'Because that's probably what I would've done if our roles had been reversed.'

It was a second or two before he answered, and he gave a little laugh. 'No you wouldn't, Juliet. You might have wanted to, but you wouldn't.'

She glanced across at him and tutted. 'Well, I certainly wouldn't have thrown myself into the lake after you. Only an idiot would do that. Don't you know you could've drowned too? Or did you happen to have a rope with you which you tied around yourself and something fixed to the ground, before you jumped in?'

He shook his head and grinned. 'No rope. I'm clearly an idiot.'

'You're definitely an idiot.'

Daphne harrumphed. 'The man just risked his life to save you, Juliet, and you call him an idiot! A thank you wouldn't go amiss.'

Juliet frowned. 'Hmm. I suppose I should thank you.'

'No need. I just did what anyone else would've done.'

She gave a little cough. 'Well. Whatever. Thank you.'

'You're very welcome. Is there anything else I can do for you?' He leant forward, a smile on his lips, a hint of devilment in his brown eyes.

'Yes.' She gingerly lifted the top of the duvet with her fingers and looked beneath it. 'You can tell me where my clothes are, and who the hell undressed me. And whose pyjamas I'm wearing. Please tell me they're not your grandad's.'

Harrison merely grinned.

'I undressed you, dear,' Daphne said. 'And your clothes are in the wash. The pyjamas are Harrison's.'

'Oh. Thank you, Daphne.' She glanced at Harrison. 'You wear pyjamas?'

'In this house, yes. I'd be a bloody fool not to. Don't worry. That pair is brand new.'

'Thank you. Er. How long will my clothes be, please, Daphne? I've got to get home for lunch.'

'You're not going anywhere,' Harrison said. 'Not until the doctor's been, at least. And I still think I should've taken you to the hospital, or called an ambulance. But Daphne said it was more important to get you warm and dry. And as she was a nurse, I've taken her word for it.'

'The nearest hospital is twenty miles away,' Daphne said. 'And an ambulance would take forever to get here in this weather.'

'That's true,' agreed Juliet. 'The snow may be melting but conditions are still bad. Cars have been abandoned at the roadside, clogging up a lot of the roads; some are impassable and the police have arranged for tow trucks to come and move them. According to the traffic report this morning.'

Harrison burst out laughing. 'Thank you, Juliet Bell for that update from your bed at The Grange. But seriously, you said your head hurt. Do you remember hitting it as you fell?'

'I don't remember anything, except falling. Then being so cold I couldn't think. And everything was dark.'

'It's probably due to the change in temperature,' Daphne said. 'But the doctor will be here any minute, I'm sure. After Harrison spoke to him, Luke drove into Mistletythe to get him because he said it would be quicker, and we know how fast that boy drives. Oh good heavens. Let's hope they haven't—'

'No,' Harrison interrupted. 'They haven't had an accident. He may drive too fast but he's a good driver.'

'Tell that to my wing mirror,' Juliet said.

Harrison coughed and got to his feet. 'Yes. Well. Today he'll be accident-free. I'd stake my life on it.'

'Have you got a death wish?' Juliet joked. 'First you risk it saving me. Now you're risking it on Luke's driving.'

Harrison grinned, but his eyes held some concern. 'I'll go and see where the doctor is. My phone's knackered. It was in my pocket when I went into the lake. I'll have to use the landline again. Oh. And we've called your family but had to leave a message because the answerphone picked up.'

'My family? Oh God. You know they'll be banging the door down the minute they get your message, don't you? That'll please your grandad.'

'I expect he'll invite them to take tea. Now don't move. I'll be back in a minute.' He pointed a finger at Juliet.

'Don't tell me what to do. But I can't go far, can I? Unless I want people to see me running around the streets in your pyjamas.'

He raised his brows. 'Now there's an image that'll be with me for the rest of the day. I'll leave Juliet in your capable hands, Daphne.'

Before Juliet could say anything else, he had gone.

Chapter Thirteen

'Are you okay?' Zoe perched on the edge of the bed and took Juliet's hand in hers. 'Mum and Dad are talking to Harrison and the doctor. They'll be in, in a minute.'

'This is ridiculous. Anyone would think I'm at death's door the way that man's behaving. I'm not allowed to move. I've got to get some sleep. I've got to keep warm. I've got to tell him if I'm feeling confused or dizzy. I'm not to be left alone. I've got to drink hot, sugared water, no caffeine. The list goes on and on.'

'Well, he's a doctor, so you should listen to him.'

'That wasn't the doctor who said all that. It was Harrison. The doctor told me I'm fine, more or less. Just a touch of mild hypothermia but my temperature's normal now and so is my heart rate, so nothing to worry about. I had a headache but that's gone and I feel absolutely fine. No ill effects as far as he can see and no reason why I shouldn't be up and about again very soon. But Harrison's insisting I stay here the night. Can you believe it? The nerve of the man.'

Zoe tutted. 'Just who does he think he is, eh? I mean, he only saved your life at the risk of his own. And he was in that water too, but is he tucked up in bed with everyone running around making sure he's okay? No. He's running around making sure you're okay. You're right. The man's got a bloody cheek.' Zoe burst out laughing. 'I think you need to stop and think, sis.'

'Oh bloody hell. You're right. It didn't even cross my mind. What a horrible person I am! He should be resting too. Do me a favour, Zoe. Please go and tell the doctor to give Harrison a once-over. I don't know much about hypothermia but I think you can get delayed shock or something and if you overdo things, it could affect your heart. But I might be wrong. Tell Harrison he's got to go and lie down. And keep warm. And do all the things he said I must do. Quick. The last thing I need right now is for that man to drop down dead because of me.'

'Okay, I'm going. But I don't think for one minute, Harrison will take much notice of me.'

Zoe hurried to the door and closed it behind her, so Juliet couldn't hear what was going on. But she did hear Harrison's slightly raised voice at one point, say: 'Oh, she did, did she?' But that was all she heard until her mum and dad came in, followed by Zoe.

'Sweetheart.' Rosa rushed to her bed and took her hands in hers. 'Oh darling, we were so worried when we heard. You father was vacuuming. Yes. Don't look so shocked. He was. Anyway. We didn't hear the phone above the noise and it was only when Cinnamon started barking maniacally that we realised something was wrong. I swear that dog has a sixth sense you know. Delayed, but it's there. But we didn't know what was wrong and it was a good five or ten minutes until we finally saw the message light flashing. By that time, Luke had dropped the doctor here and come back down to call on us. Zoe let him in just as we were playing Harrison's message. Not that any of that matters now. The doctor says you'll be fine. I can't tell you what a relief that is, sweetheart.'

'Luke came to tell you?'

'Yes, darling. He drove us here in his car. It took less than a minute. At least it felt like that.'

Juliet couldn't help but laugh, although she wasn't quite sure why. The whole thing seemed so farcical, and yet it could have been a very different story. If Harrison hadn't been at the lake at the exact same time as she was, she might well be dead. And that was definitely not something to laugh about.

But it was something to think about.

Why was he there at that precise time?

Luke said he wouldn't tell Harrison. Was it pure coincidence? Or Fate?

She glanced at Zoe and suddenly, she thought she knew the answer.

Yesterday, Zoe and Luke had 'arranged' for them all to be at Merry's Christmas Tree Farm at the same time. Had Zoe and Luke 'arranged' for Harrison to be at the lake at exactly the same time as her? And if so, why? Harrison was with Kiki, wasn't he? Would Luke really try to set his brother up with someone else under the very nose of the man's girlfriend?

'Is there anything you need, sweetheart?' Bernard was asking.

'What, Dad? Oh. Sorry. No, I'm fine thanks. Daphne – and Harrison – have made sure I've got everything, thanks. I'm sorry I've dragged you all back here under such ridiculous circumstances.'

'Nothing to be sorry about, sweetheart.' Bernard gently tapped her hand. 'Harrison has been extremely kind and considerate. He says we should feel free to go wherever we want and to stay as long as we like. He's even having a room made up so that your mother can stay here tonight.'

'What?' Juliet couldn't believe her ears. 'There's no need for any of us to stay here tonight. I'll get a couple of hours' sleep and then this evening, Zoe can come and get me and bring me home. You don't mind, Zoe, do you?'

Zoe shook her head. 'I don't mind at all. But I'm not going to do it. No. Don't shout at me. If you want to shout at anyone, shout at Harrison. He is adamant that you're not going anywhere until the morning. He even got the doctor to agree it might be wise, so you're here for the night whether you like it or not.'

'Of course you should stay,' Rosa said. 'Shock can be a very nasty thing, sweetheart. You may think you feel fine now but a delayed reaction can occur at any time and then where would we be? No. Harrison's right. He says we're all welcome to stay but your father and I think that it's best if it's just me. Harrison's going to take us home in the morning, providing you're still fine, that is.'

Juliet could hardly argue. Hadn't she told Zoe the exact same thing about delayed shock only a moment ago? And, once she got used to the idea, spending a night in her old room might actually be a treat. And one she would never get a chance to repeat. She should make the most of it. It might bring back lots of memories, but in a way, it might be cathartic. It could finally give her closure. And that wasn't such a bad thing.

She snuggled under the covers and smiled. 'Okay. If that's what everyone thinks is best, I won't argue.'

'God,' Zoe said. 'Quick. Get the doctor back. My sister is definitely ill.'

'Oh very funny,' said Juliet.

'Now, now girls,' Bernard said. But he was smiling, and so was Rosa.

Chapter Fourteen

The next time Juliet awoke, it was dark outside. Her bedroom curtains were undrawn and she could see the moon, nearly three-quarters full, through one of the two windows in the room. Its silvery beam was reflected in the full-length, antique cheval mirror in the corner of her room. That mirror had reflected her image throughout the first sixteen years of her life.

A lump formed in her throat as she saw flashes of a five-year-old, pirouetting in front of it in a pink Tutu, her favourite Unicorn toy in one hand, a Prince Charming doll in the other. An eight-year-old going to a party she didn't want to go to. A fourteen-year-old, wondering if her freckles would ever disappear. And a sixteen-year-old trying on dress after dress and tilting the mirror this way and that, to decide which to wear on her very first date with the boy she'd just met at the lake. Just a few weeks later, she looked into that mirror for what she thought would be the very last time. There wasn't room for such large, ornate furniture at 29 Mistletoe Row.

A knock on the door gave her a start.

'Come in,' she said, reaching across to switch on the bedside lamp.

Instead of her mum, or Daphne, or even Harrison, a swathe of long, sleek, mahogany hair appeared around the door, followed by a smile the size of the moon, and a soft, sultry voice said, 'Hi.'

'Hello,' Juliet replied, unable to think of anything else.

'We haven't been introduced.' The woman sashayed into the room wearing an expensive-looking and extremely short dressing gown of the finest silk Juliet had ever seen. It was loosely tied and left little to the imagination. She was evidently naked beneath. She sat serenely on the very edge of the bed, without even making an indentation, or so it seemed and crossed her long, shapely legs. 'I'm Kiki. I'm here with Harrison.'

Juliet tried not to imagine what that meant, even though she had already assumed the beautiful woman was Harrison's girlfriend. At least there was no engagement ring on her left hand.

'I'm Juliet. I'm sorry for the inconvenience my mishap has caused. Is Harrison okay?'

'No need to apologise. We hardly know you're here. And Harrison's fine. I've just left him in the shower. I thought I'd pop in before we dressed and went downstairs for drinks. Is there anything you need?'

Juliet cleared her throat. But she couldn't clear the image of Harrison and this beautiful woman in the shower together, quite so easily. And that was clearly what Kiki was telling her. She shook her head. 'No thanks. Mum's bringing a tray up later.'

'You were so lucky Harrison had decided to go for a walk this morning.' She leant forward and brushed Juliet's arm with long, slim fingers and red-painted nails. 'I was still in bed. Ask Harrison. I'm not a morning person.'

'At eleven o'clock?' It must have been around eleven when she crashed through the ice. She'd been skating for quite some time beforehand. 'That's almost lunchtime.'

Kiki smiled. 'What can I say? We went to the local pub last night and had such a good time, we didn't get home till late. And Harrison's … well, let's just say, Harrison's very active.' She yawned and stretched like a panther before giggling like a naughty little girl. 'And a girl's got to get some sleep if she wants to stay beautiful, hasn't she?'

She looked Juliet up and down. Not that she would be able to see anything, other than the top of Harrison's pyjamas, but Juliet still pulled the duvet up towards her chin.

'You're certainly very beautiful,' Juliet said. 'Have … have you and Harrison been together long?'

'Why thank you, Juliet. That's so sweet of you. And your freckles are really cute. Goodness. Sometimes it feels as if we've been together forever. He and my brother Charlie are the best of friends. But it's only been four years. We work together too. I've known Luke for years, of course, but I'm here to meet their grandfather. Do you know him? I hear you lived here once. Before you and your family fell on hard times. I feel for you. That must be awful to come from a house such as this and end up in a tiny little cottage. So very sad.'

Juliet was enraged, but she forced a smile. 'I have wonderful memories of this house, but we were only saying yesterday that none of us miss the upkeep of this place. The draughts, the smoky chimneys, rattling windows and such. The cottage is so warm and cosy. We love it there. In fact, I love it so much I'm actually moving back. I've been living and working in Bristol since I went to uni there. But my heart will always be in Mistletythe, and Mistletoe Row in particular. As for Rufus. Yes, I know him, but I haven't seen him for years, and I can't say I'm sorry about it. I don't want to seem rude, but I'm really very tired. And Harrison insisted I get plenty of sleep.'

The smile on Kiki's lips wavered momentarily but it was soon set back to stun. Or perhaps Juliet was judging her too harshly. Perhaps the smile wasn't as false as it looked.

'Of course. And he said the same to me. "We need to make sure she gets plenty of sleep, so that she can leave tomorrow," were his words to me before he sent me in here. Sweet dreams, Juliet. We'll raise a glass of champagne to you feeling better. Lovely to meet you.'

'And you, Kiki. Good night.'

Juliet heard the door close tight as Kiki left the room.

'And good riddance. You may be beautiful, but I think you're a bit of a bitch.'

Chapter Fifteen

'You're leaving?' Harrison hoped that hadn't sounded as desperate to her as it had to him.

Juliet smiled as she and Rosa met him at the foot of the stairs. 'Yes. Thank you so, so much for everything, but I'm feeling absolutely fine this morning, after a good night's sleep, and we really don't want to be in the way.'

'You're not. Not in the slightest. Please don't feel you have to go, because you don't.'

'That's kind of you. But the truth is, we want to go home.'

Juliet's smile looked as if it took some effort. Did she still hate him so much? He thought they had broken the ice yesterday. In more ways than one. Clearly, he was wrong.

'Mrs Bell, are you sure? Honestly, you're both very welcome here. And as I said yesterday, so is the rest of your family. You can even bring your dog. Cinnamon, isn't it? Please don't rush off on our account.'

Rosa smiled, more genuinely than Juliet, he felt. 'Harrison, you've been so kind and thoughtful. But we really do want to be at home. I'm sure you understand. It's Christmas. We've still got so much to do, and what with Juliet moving home permanently. Well, maybe not permanently but certainly until she gets another job, we—'

'Harrison doesn't want to hear all that, Mum. Come along. Zoe will be outside, I'm sure.'

'You … you're moving back?'

She ignored him and headed towards the front door.

'You've called Zoe to come and get you?' He wasn't sure what was happening, or how it was happening so fast.

'Yes. Thank Luke and Daphne, will you, please? I'll thank them again when I see them. Oh. And say goodbye to Kiki, for me. I know she'll still be in bed.'

'Yes. She will. She's definitely not a morning person.'

Something flashed across Juliet's face, but it was gone before he could see exactly what it was. She didn't look happy though.

'Well. It was lovely to meet her, but I doubt we'll meet again. Goodbye Harrison. And thanks again for everything. I hope you have a very happy Christmas.'

'I'll see you again before Christmas, won't I?'

Juliet didn't reply. She simply smiled and marched to the door.

'Goodbye, Harrison,' Rosa said. 'Do pop in and say hello if you're passing.'

'Mum!'

Juliet definitely wasn't happy. Was it something he had done?

Or hadn't done?

And when had she met Kiki? Kiki hadn't mentioned it. She had told him that she had knocked on the door before dinner and that Juliet was sound asleep and snoring. She'd turned her nose up, as if a woman snoring was a big no-no, and he'd laughed and said he couldn't imagine that, but so what if she did? Lots of people snored.

'I don't,' Kiki had replied.

Juliet must have been extremely tired because on both occasions he had knocked on the door and poked his head round, she had been fast asleep. He could hear her rhythmic breathing and when he'd softly called her name, she hadn't responded.

She hadn't been snoring, either.

Something was nagging at him, but he wasn't sure what.

He followed Juliet and Rosa outside and Zoe pulled up as he reached them.

'Please pop back whenever you like. Or if you want to walk around the grounds or anything, please feel free to do so. I'd avoid skating on the lake for a while though.' He gave a little laugh, but

Juliet threw him an odd look as if she didn't find it funny. 'But come up and walk around it, or sit on the bench whenever you like. I'll tell Luke and Daphne you've got my permission.'

'I'm not sure your grandad would be pleased,' Juliet said, without looking at him.

'He won't mind. But it makes no difference if he does.'

'Well, we won't, so there's no need to worry about it. Thank you though. Goodbye.'

'Hi Harrison,' Zoe said, getting out of the car and helping Juliet to get in to the back.

'Hello, Zoe.' He smiled at her and she smiled back.

Rosa sat on the front passenger seat and waved as Zoe got in and they pulled away. Juliet didn't smile. She didn't wave. She didn't even look at him.

Had yesterday all been a dream? He was sure they had been getting on. He even thought they could, perhaps, be friends. He hoped they could be more, in time. Why had it all gone so wrong?

Again.

He stood and watched the car until the tail lights disappeared behind their cottage on Mistletoe Row.

Shivering, he turned and went upstairs, opening the door to her room. The Rose room. The bed was made and his pyjamas were neatly folded on the pillow. He walked over, sat on the bed and picked them up. Rather foolishly he hugged them to him.

Would it be too ridiculous to never wash them again?

He gave a self-deprecating laugh. God. He was beyond all hope.

He shook his head. He'd throw them in the wash himself. He had really got to get over her.

Seriously. Twenty years was quite long enough to harbour any hope for something that was clearly never going to be.

'Get a grip, Harrison,' he told himself, as he got up and left the room, closing the door behind him.

Chapter Sixteen

'Okay,' Zoe said, as she and Juliet sat on the sofa in the sitting room, drinking hot chocolate and eating mince pies, straight from the oven. 'Why do you keep giving me funny looks? You've been doing it ever since we got back from The Grange, and that was hours ago.'

'Did you and Luke do anything?'

Zoe's cheeks flushed, but she was sitting near the fire and the logs were roaring as the flames leapt high into the throat of the chimney. 'Like what?'

'Like telling Harrison I'd be ice skating yesterday morning around ten o'clock. Or perhaps, suggesting he go to the lake for some reason or another.'

'Why would we do that?'

'You tell me. That's precisely what I'd like to know.'

'What makes you think it had anything to do with us? Perhaps he simply decided to go for a walk to the lake yesterday morning.'

'Perhaps he did. And I'm very glad he was there, believe me. But it is a bit of a coincidence, isn't it? I mean, you did admit that you and Luke arranged for us all to be at Merry's Christmas Tree Farm at the same time. Is it too much of a stretch to wonder if you arranged for me and Harrison to be at the lake at the same time?'

Zoe sighed. 'Oh, okay. It was us. Luke told Harrison he had seen something on the lake and he wasn't sure what it was. He knew Harrison would go and investigate. But you must admit, you loved being on the lake again, didn't you? Until you fell through the ice, of course.'

Juliet laughed, in spite of the situation. 'Yes. I'll admit I was in absolute heaven until I dropped like a stone into that freezing water.'

Zoe shivered. 'Actually, it doesn't bear thinking about does it? What could've happened, I mean. Just imagine if Harrison hadn't gone. No one would've seen you fall through the ice. No one would've been there to rescue you. Bloody hell, sis. You might have drowned. And it would've been my fault. I'm so sorry. I truly am.'

'Hey.' Juliet reached out a hand and rubbed Zoe's knee. 'Don't beat yourself up about it. Harrison came, he saw, he saved me.' She gave a little laugh. 'That's got a certain ring to it. Anyway. The point is, it all ended well. And I even got a bonus. I got to spend a night in my old room again. And I never, ever imagined that would happen. It was well worth almost drowning for.'

'Was it weird? Being in your room again?'

'Yes and no. It's just the same as it was and I'm not sure whether that was good or bad. I know I didn't want to leave this morning.'

'Then why did you? Harrison said you could've stayed.'

'I didn't want to stay, either. I know that sounds crazy, and I can't explain. I think perhaps I was worried I might not ever want to leave. Better to get out whilst I could. Being dragged out of the house kicking and screaming wouldn't be a good look. Especially as it wouldn't be the first time.'

'You didn't exactly kick and scream when we moved out. Not that I can remember, anyway.'

'Not on the actual day, perhaps. But there was a lot of kicking and screaming leading up to it, I promise you. Part of that was to do with Harrison, though. Because I thought he'd lied to me. And part of it was because I was so angry with myself. Anyway, what's done is done. I won't be going there again.'

'Never?'

Juliet shrugged. 'There's no reason to.'

'But … Aren't you and Harrison friends now? Or at least on speaking terms?'

'I suppose so. But to be honest, I'll be happy once he's gone. And I hope I don't see him much while he's here.'

'Why not?'

'Oh Zoe. I really can't explain. I just think it would be better for everyone if Harrison and I kept our distance. Why were you trying to throw us together, by the way?'

'Ah. I'm not sure you're going to like this.'

'Try me.'

Zoe smiled and leant forward. 'You know I told you that Luke and I are friends?'

'Y-es.'

'Well the truth is … We're a bit more than friends. A lot more than friends, actually. Oh, I might as well just say it, because it's got to come out sooner or later. Luke and I are dating. It'll be six months at Christmas.'

'What?' Juliet was astonished.

'That was why it was so important to us that you and Harrison get on. Things are serious between us and we're tired of keeping it quiet. Of hiding it from everyone. I haven't even told Mum and Dad. And that makes me feel terrible. But I didn't want to tell them without telling you, and besides, if I told Mum, she'd be on the phone to you immediately. So I had to keep it secret. And Luke hasn't told anyone either. Not Harrison, or his grandad. That's why Luke asked Harrison to come for Christmas. He plans to tell him now.'

'Wow. I don't know what to say. How have you managed to date for six months without anyone finding out? I'm astonished. You deserve a medal. Where do you go on your dates? Or shouldn't I ask?'

Zoe sighed. 'We go to the cinema, and restaurants, and pubs, just like any other couple. But we have to drive to somewhere like Michaelmas Bay, or Snowflake Cove, where we're not so well known. Although we did see Robin Merry once, shortly after he started dating Raven. They were in Snowflake Inn and we'd gone there for a drink. I swore him to secrecy, and he was pretty understanding. In the summer, we had lots of picnics in the grounds of The Grange. Luke knows Daphne's routine, so we knew we wouldn't be seen. But we're in love, and we want everyone to know we're a couple. I know it might be hard on you, and Mum and Dad. But we didn't plan to fall in love. These things just happen.'

'Don't I know it. Oh, Zoe. I'm happy for you. I'm happy for you both. I just hope his grandad and Harrison feel the same.'

'I don't think Harrison will be a problem. And Luke says he doesn't care what his grandad thinks. But I'm pretty sure he does. I just have to hope the old man accepts me. It's not as if Luke is going to inherit the house or anything, so I won't be moving back in, if our relationship runs the course. And that's something else Luke is going to talk to Harrison about during this holiday. Luke and I are planning to start a business together.'

134

'What?' There was one surprise after another, and Juliet wasn't sure how many more she could take. 'A business? What sort of business?'

'A property business, like Harrison's. Only smaller. Luke hates his job in the city. He hates commuting. He hates designing buildings only to be told they're not quite what the company had in mind. He's always been good with his hands and as an architect, he's got a lot of knowledge others haven't. And I've always been good with interior design. So basically, he'll redesign, renovate and rebuild the structure as necessary, and I'll design and style the interiors. I'll keep my secretarial job in Mistletythe until we've got some money coming in. But Luke is thirty in February, and just like Harrison did, Luke will get his trust fund monies on his thirtieth birthday. I don't know how much it is, but it should help us get started. Oh, and we're calling the business, Bells & Bows Building & Design.'

For a moment, Juliet was speechless. She stared at her younger sister in disbelief. Zoe stared back, a little nervously. And then Juliet put her half full mug of chocolate on the side table and jumped to her feet, pulling Zoe up and hugging her tight.

'Oh, Zoe. I'm so happy for you. Truly, truly happy. I wish you every success. You deserve it. But I think you'd better tell Mum and Dad. There have been enough secrets and misunderstandings in this family to last a lifetime. And we did all promise to work on our communication skills. The sooner you tell them the better.'

'I know. You're right. I'll tell them right now. Hey, sis. It won't be too dreadful being Luke's sister-in-law, will it? He hasn't asked me yet, but I'm pretty sure he will. And I'm going to say yes.'

Juliet laughed. 'Of course you're going to say yes. And no. It won't be too dreadful. And now that Harrison's saved my life, I suppose I should try and be nice to him. I just wish his girlfriend wasn't quite so awful.'

Zoe held Juliet at arm's length. 'Girlfriend? Harrison doesn't have a girlfriend. At least, not one Luke's heard of.'

'Yes he has. It's Kiki.'

'Kiki?' Now it was Zoe who looked astonished. 'Harrison's dating Kiki? That's the first I've heard of it. And Luke definitely doesn't know. He told me Kiki is Harrison's executive assistant. She has been for the last four years. Harrison knows her brother, apparently, and when his last assistant decided not to return from maternity leave, Kiki stepped in temporarily. But they get on really well, workwise, so he offered her a permanent position.'

'Precisely.'

'No. A permanent job. Not a permanent relationship.'

'Well, I can assure you, they're definitely having a relationship. She came into my room last night, fresh from having sex with him in the shower. And she told me herself that they're a couple. That's why she's here. To meet Harrison's grandad. So it must be fairly serious.'

'Bloody hell. Luke honestly doesn't know that. I wonder if Harrison's going to tell him? Perhaps that's why Harrison agreed to come back for Christmas when Luke asked him. Maybe Luke isn't the only one making plans for the future. Maybe Harrison has some plans of his own.'

The thought of Harrison making plans with Kiki made Juliet feel a bit sick.

'I think delayed shock may be kicking in,' she said. 'I'm feeling dizzy. You go and tell Mum and Dad your news. I'm going to go to bed. Wake me in time for dinner, please. Although I'm not sure I could eat a thing the way I feel right now.'

Chapter Seventeen

Thursday was as beautiful, weather-wise, as Wednesday had been. The sun was shining, the sky was a cloudless baby blue, and it was warm again for the time of year. Harrison walked down to the lake and brushed the small amount of remaining snow from the bench. There wasn't even a frost this morning, and the snow on the ground was rapidly turning to a coffee coloured slush.

The last few days had been a complete shock to his system. Juliet had walked back into his life at Merry's Christmas Tree Farm on Monday, nearly drowned on Tuesday — but given him a small amount of hope — and walked back out of it on Wednesday.

And as if that wasn't bad enough, Luke had spent Wednesday afternoon telling him his own plans for the future, which astonishingly involved Juliet's younger sister, Zoe.

If Luke's relationship progressed with Zoe the way Luke seemed positive it would, Juliet would be in Harrison's life forever. Only not in the way he wanted. So close, and yet so far.

It would be inevitable that they would meet at family gatherings; he couldn't avoid them all. For the past twenty years he had managed to evade spending Christmas with his grandfather, but he had always spent time with Luke over the holidays, and seen him on birthdays and several times throughout each year. If Luke set up home with Zoe, Harrison could hardly ask him to spend those times at Harrison's home, and not his own with his wife, and possibly her family. And then of course, Luke and Zoe would have a family of their own, to whom he would be an uncle and Juliet, an aunt. There was some irony in that.

He was happy for Luke, of course. Luke had found love and someone to share his life with; something Harrison had failed miserably at. His love was unrequited and had been for twenty years. But he wasn't going to think about that yet again.

Once Harrison had recovered from the shock of Luke's news, he and Luke had spent Wednesday evening discussing Luke and Zoe's potential business. Luke would receive the money from his trust fund on his thirtieth birthday, and that was a couple of hundred thousand pounds. More than enough to start a new venture. But his birthday wasn't until February and Harrison could see how enthusiastic Luke was and how keen to get the ball rolling. Luke had only asked for Harrison's advice, and for some moral support to help him and Zoe get the business off the ground. Harrison had offered to give Luke the start-up money as a Christmas and early birthday present. That meant they could begin their future together right away. Luke had jumped at the chance.

When Harrison had turned thirty, he had come into his trust fund, but he had already started a business, years before, and made plenty of money of his own. As the eldest son, Harrison had not only received more money than Luke, he had also inherited an ancient family trust – and that now included The Grange. And that was when he had discovered the full extent of his grandfather's deception.

If he could have hated the old man more, he would have. Instead, what he discovered had actually made him feel sad for Rufus Bow.

Rufus hadn't purchased The Grange with his own money twenty years ago; he had used money that had actually belonged to Harrison. Well, to Harrison from the ancient family trust, and money from Harrison's own father, who, prior to his death, had made Rufus executor of his will, a trustee of his estate, and given power of attorney. Which basically had meant that the million or so Harrison's father had made from running his own extremely successful housebuilding business, together with a couple of million from the ancient trust, had been sitting in a bank account for Rufus to use however he wished – the only proviso being that it must be to Harrison's future benefit. Strictly speaking, Rufus had never owned The Grange. It had always belonged to Harrison. He simply hadn't known about it until his thirtieth birthday.

And when, eight years ago, he had discovered the truth, he had been sorely tempted to kick the old man out without a penny. At least, without a penny of Harrison's money. Rufus did have money of his own, simply nowhere near as many zeros as Harrison. Instead, Harrison had merely decided he would never speak to the old man again. Not that they had spoken much since the day Harrison left The Grange as an unhappy and resentful eighteen-year-old. The only thing they had discussed during all those years had been Luke, and what was best for Luke's future.

The one thing Harrison had never understood was why Rufus was so hell-bent on owning The Grange. He had a perfectly good home of his own. And so had Harrison's parents. Maybe neither house had been as grand as The Grange, and certainly nowhere near as old, but they had both been fairly impressive. Rufus had sold both houses.

It had only been about three years or so ago, and then by pure chance, that Harrison had uncovered Rufus' final secret. And he had certainly kept it a secret. Rufus' father, Harrison's great-grandfather, had been engaged to Juliet's great-grandmother, and apparently been madly in love. Madly, being the appropriate word. It seemed the man was a bit of a tyrant, to put it mildly, and his fiancée had second thoughts. She broke the engagement off, which caused substantial embarrassment to the Bows, apparently. But who could blame her? Even Harrison had heard stories of how truly evil his great-grandfather had been. Well, the man certainly blamed Juliet's great-grandmother, and also the woman's father for not forcing his daughter to honour her engagement. And he swore that one day he, or one of the Bows, would own The Grange. Even after he married Harrison's unfortunate great-grandmother and had Rufus, the man had been obsessed. Rufus had spent his childhood and long after, constantly hearing that one day, the Bows would own The Grange.

But Harrison's great-grandfather hadn't been the first Bow to want the place. The Bows had wanted it for hundreds of years before. That was another thing Harrison had discovered three years ago when he had finally taken the time to go through all the old papers, records, letters and diaries he had also inherited on his thirtieth birthday.

The revelation had unnerved him, almost as much as when he had uncovered Rufus' deception. It had also made him question his long-held feelings for Juliet. Was there some rogue gene or something in the Bow family that drew them all to the Bells and to The Grange? It was more than a little worrying. Or perhaps something in the Bows was repeatedly attracted to something in the Bells. Perhaps the families were actually meant to be together.

That thought made him laugh out loud. It wasn't his fault he was still in love with Juliet; it was simply in his blood.

And now his younger brother Luke had succumbed. He too had fallen in love with a Bell. It was like a virus. Well, scientists had always said that falling in love was merely a chemical reaction – a biological drive. Did that make the situation better, or worse? And did it even matter? He had fallen in love with Juliet. Luke had fallen in love with Zoe. At least one of them would have a happy ending.

Harrison spent the morning walking around the grounds, and eventually, once Kiki was up, dressed and ready for action, they had had lunch and then spent the afternoon working. He wanted to get the ball rolling with regard to the finances for Luke before the banks, the lawyers, and the accountants shut down for the Christmas holiday.

To say that Kiki was astonished regarding Luke and Zoe, was possibly an understatement.

'What is it with that bloody family?' she said.

Harrison laughed. 'I've been asking myself that question all morning. I blame the universe. We're all made up of stardust. Perhaps, billions of years ago, the Bow's stardust and the Bell's stardust were part of the same star, and we've spent billions of years trying to reform.'

'What? Have you started drinking early? I know it's the festive season and I've seen your grandfather with a glass in his hand at eleven a.m. but consuming alcohol before seven in the evening is a first for you.'

'No, Kiki. I haven't been drinking. But I suppose you could say I am a little punch-drunk. There's been one surprise after another since I got here.'

'You can say that again.'

He did have several glasses of wine with dinner, and a brandy or two after that, but by the time he went to bed, he began to wish he hadn't. Kiki had been getting a little tactile all evening and as they walked upstairs she linked her arm through his.

'We haven't spent much time together, have we? Just you and me, I mean.'

'No. There hasn't been much time for work, I agree.'

Kiki tutted. 'I wasn't talking about work, Harrison. I was talking about us. I was hoping we could spend more time getting to know one another. That's one of the reasons I came here.'

Harrison furrowed his brows. 'We do know one another.'

'Oh, Harrison. I mean, I was hoping that there might be more to our relationship than work. And please don't say we're friends. Or that I'm like a sister to you. I don't want to be your sister, Harrison. And I want to be so much more than your friend. Can't you see how I feel about you? Don't you find me attractive?'

'Of course I do. Any man would. You're gorgeous, Kiki.'

'So?'

He hesitated. 'Er. So … What?'

'Are you being intentionally obtuse?'

'I'm not being intentionally anything. I'm not sure what you're saying.'

'I'm saying I'm attracted to you, Harrison. Sexually attracted. I'm saying I want to go to bed with you. To have sex with you. To have a relationship with you. Wouldn't you like that?'

'Er.'

'Er? What do you mean, "Er"? Is that all you have to say? Jesus, Harrison. I'm offering myself to you on a plate. What more do I have to do?'

Harrison gave a little cough, ran his free hand through his hair, and sighed deeply as he turned to face her at the top of the stairs.

'I'm sorry, Kiki. I don't know what else to say. You're gorgeous. And I'll admit the thought of us having more than a working relationship has crossed my mind once or twice. But the plain fact is, I don't have those sort of feelings for you. I don't love you, Kiki. I like you a lot, but that isn't enough. Not for me at least.'

'That's nonsense. Complete and utter nonsense. Are you telling me that you've been in love with all the other women you've gone to bed with? We both know there have been a few.'

'No. In fact, I don't think I've been in love with any of them. Not really in love, in any event. But it's different with you.'

'Why?'

'Because with those women, I saw them, I was attracted to them and things progressed naturally from there. I didn't know them beforehand. I wasn't friends with any of them. If you and I slept together now, it would probably ruin our friendship. It would definitely affect our working relationship. We couldn't just have a casual affair. And I can't offer you anything else. We don't have a future together, Kiki. Not as husband and wife.'

'Why do we need to be husband and wife?'

'Because that's what I want for my future. I want someone I can share it with.'

'You can share it with me.'

He shook his head and lowered his eyes. 'No, Kiki. I can't.'

'Well then, let's not worry about the future. Let's just have fun tonight, and for several nights to come.' She laughed seductively and wrapped her arms around his neck.

He sighed deeply and with his hands, he removed her arms, and held her hands in his. He looked into her eyes and smiled wanly, shaking his head. 'No, Kiki. It wouldn't be fair, and that would stop it from being fun.'

'You don't know what you're missing, Harrison.'

He gave a light-hearted laugh. 'Oh I think I do. And I may very well kick myself for it in time. But for now I must do what's best for both of us. And going to bed with you is not what's best for you, or for me. Good night, Kiki. And pleasant dreams. Let's both forget we had this conversation in the morning.'

'Huh! And pleasant dreams to you, Harrison. Why any man would want to spend his nights alone when he could be in bed with me, is beyond my comprehension.'

'It's beyond mine, too. But that's the way it is.'

She turned and marched down the hall to the Dawn room and slammed the door behind her.

Chapter Eighteen

The weather wasn't the only thing that had turned distinctly frosty on Friday morning. Kiki's smile was made of ice, which matched the look in her green eyes. Over breakfast, for which Kiki had uncharacteristically got up early, she smiled warmly and laughed with Luke, but every time Harrison opened his mouth, his words were met with an arctic blast. He couldn't really blame her. He knew how it felt to tell someone you loved them and to have it thrown back in your face. Not that Kiki had said she loved him, exactly, and neither had he thrown it in her face, but a line had clearly been crossed, and he wasn't sure they would ever come back across it.

'Zoe and I are going Christmas shopping in town today,' Luke said, seemingly unaware of the tension in the air. 'Would you and Kiki like to join us?'

Harrison shook his head. 'Thanks for the offer, but I've got a lot of documents I need to read and sign before everyone closes for Christmas. And it's Christmas Eve on Monday, so I'm running out of time. I won't be needing you though, Kiki, so if you want to join Luke and Zoe, that's fine.'

'Thank you so much, Harrison,' she said, and he could almost see the words freezing in the air, despite the heating being on full pelt and the warmth emanating from the roaring fire in the dining room. Her stare was equally frosty. 'But if you don't mind, I'll stay here. I have a few calls to make and emails to send. I'm considering a career change.'

Harrison wasn't completely surprised, but Luke appeared to be.

'A career change?' He looked from one to the other. 'Have you two had a row or something? It's not about me, is it? Or my new business, because I'd hate to think I've said or done anything to cause a rift between you.'

'It's nothing you've said or done, Luke,' Harrison said, smiling at him. 'It's all my fault. I've been thoughtless and inconsiderate, as usual. But a career change might not be a bad thing, Kiki. Although I'd miss you dreadfully and I know I'll struggle to find a replacement anywhere near as good as you.'

'I know,' she said, giving him an even icier stare.

'What's going on?' Luke asked. 'What's happened? Surely you can work this out.'

'I'm not sure we can.' Harrison finished his coffee. 'I hope we'll remain friends though. Good friends. And, of course, you'll still be staying for Christmas, won't you? Unless you'd prefer to get a flight to Aspen and join Charlie. I can arrange that if that's what you'd prefer.'

'Again, so kind. Let me get back to you on that.'

Harrison shrugged. 'Sure. Anytime. You know where to find me.'

'Oh yes. I know exactly where to find you. So Luke, have you actually proposed to Zoe, or are you waiting to see how things develop?'

Luke laughed. 'I haven't officially proposed, but we both know we're headed for the altar. And in the not too distant future, I should think. I was waiting to see how Harrison took the news before making it official.'

'Why? What did it matter what Harrison thought? You're your own man, Luke, and you'll soon be a very wealthy one. Are you saying you would have tossed the girl aside if Harrison hadn't approved?'

'God no! That wasn't what I meant. It's just that, there's been some bad blood between our families and I wanted to know I had Harrison's blessing before I asked. I would still propose though, even without it. But I wanted to tell him it was something I was planning to do rather than tell him it was done and he had to live with it.'

'I don't see the difference.'

'What Luke means is that he wanted to give me time to get used to the idea, I think, rather than just hit me in the face with it. I respect and admire him for that. And Zoe, too, for understanding.'

'Aw. How sweet. And Juliet will be over the moon that she'll finally get her house back. It won't be hers, of course, but with her sister married to a Bow, and no doubt living here, she'll get to come and go as and when she pleases, won't she? And I know how much that will mean to her. I've heard a bit about it from Daphne, your grandfather, and the locals. It seems there's a whole history between the Bells and the Bows.'

'Yes,' Harrison said, his fingers clutching the handle of his empty coffee cup. 'And now there's going to be an entire future between our families, too. But I'm not sure Juliet will exactly be over the moon about it.'

'She's fine with it,' said Luke, smiling at his brother. 'Zoe told her on Wednesday when they got home. Just before I told you. She was shocked, of course. But Zoe said Juliet was genuinely pleased for us. And she's going to be a bridesmaid when we do get married. Zoe's already told her that.'

'Then I think it's about time you actually proposed,' Harrison said, grinning. 'It seems a bit non-sensical to be planning a wedding before you've asked the question. Even if you both know the answer will be yes. Have you spoken to the old man?'

Luke tutted and shook his head. 'I told him last night. He wasn't best pleased, but I made it clear that it's happening, regardless, and that he can choose to either be a part of our lives, or not. I'm glad to say, he chose to be a part of it, albeit rather grudgingly.'

'Then that's the final hurdle jumped. Have you got the money for a ring?'

Luke laughed. 'Yes thanks. I'd have asked you for a loan for that if I hadn't, don't worry. But I've been saving for a while now and I'm going to get her something really fantastic.'

'If you want any help with that,' Kiki said, reaching out her hand and brushing Luke's fingers with hers. 'I've got excellent taste in jewellery. I can show you exactly what she'll want. The more diamonds the better and at least 5 carats for the central one. I assume you can stretch to that.'

'Thanks,' Luke replied. 'But I've got a pretty good idea of what Zoe likes and doesn't like. And actually, she'd prefer something simple. She's really not into ostentatious jewellery, even engagements rings. She joked that she didn't want anything too big or heavy because it would be on her finger for at least eighty years and when she gets arthritis, she doesn't want a ring that'll break her weak and ageing bones.'

Harrison laughed. 'That's the sort of thing Juliet would say.'

Luke grinned. 'Yeah. She and Zoe are so alike, and yet so different. Zoe's really happy that Juliet's come home. She says they're already closer than they've ever been and she's loving having a big sister she can talk to about anything. Everything seems to be falling into place. It's almost as if all this was meant to be.'

'Pre-ordained, you mean?' Harrison asked.

'Yes, exactly.'

Kiki rolled her eyes. 'Dear God. You two are like a couple of teenage girls! Next you'll be saying you both believe in Father Christmas. Or... or Unicorns.' Kiki slapped her napkin on the table and slumped back in her chair.

Luke raised his brows. 'Juliet believes in Unicorns. Or she did. I remember Zoe telling me.'

Kiki glowered at Harrison. 'Unicorns. Hmm. That explains a lot. Excuse me, please. I have some calls to make.'

'What's up with her?' Luke asked, as she slammed the door behind her. 'What's really happened between you?'

Harrison got to his feet. 'Nothing, Luke. Honestly. Just a little misunderstanding of what we want from the future. Please don't worry about it. But if Zoe wants a job as my assistant, please let me know. I'd better get to those papers. They won't sign themselves.'

Luke laughed. 'I think Zoe will stay put for now. At least until we get our business up and running. But thanks for the offer.'

Harrison was about to close the door when Luke added: 'Oh. But I do know someone who is looking for a job. And she was an executive assistant, I believe.'

'Oh? Who's that?' Harrison turned back to look at Luke.

'Juliet. She's been made redundant. That's why she's moving back. She's planning to work in London if she can't get anything local.'

Harrison nearly choked. 'I can't see Juliet wanting to work for me, can you? We may be speaking – just about, but I think she'd rather throw herself back in the lake than be my assistant. And besides, I need to concentrate on work. With Juliet sitting the other side of my desk, all I'd be thinking about would be leaping across it, throwing her on it and making mad, passionate love to her.'

'Shit, Harrison! I knew it. I knew you were head over heels in love with her. That's why you've asked about her constantly over the years. Not merely out of interest because you were friends once, as you claimed. Why the hell didn't you say something sooner?'

He shook his head. 'I can't believe I've actually said it now.' He ran a hand through his hair. 'Do me a massive favour, Luke, and keep that to yourself. She really doesn't have any interest in me at all, and with you and Zoe getting married, I'd hate for there to be even more tension between Juliet and me than there is already.'

'But if you told her how you feel—'

'No, Luke! I'm serious. Don't say one word to her. I never thought I'd hear myself say this – and doing so makes me feel a little bit sick. I'm clearly more like the old man than I want to admit. But if you want my help and the funds to start your business, you'll promise me now, you won't tell Juliet what I just said. Or that I have any feelings for her whatsoever. Is that clear?'

'Jesus, Harrison. Yes that's clear. But I think you're making a mistake.'

'It won't be my first and I doubt it'll be my last. I'm sorry, Luke. But this is really important to me. Please promise me.'

'Okay. I promise. I won't say one word to Juliet about the way you feel. Not *one* word.'

Harrison breathed a sigh of relief. 'Thank you, Luke. That means a lot.'

He smiled and closed the door, feeling grateful that his brother had agreed to his demand, but feeling dreadful that he'd made it, and furious with himself that now all he could think about was Juliet on his desk and what he'd like to do. Not many papers were going to get signed at this rate. And there were only two working days until Christmas, counting today and Christmas Eve.

And now he'd also got to find himself another bloody assistant. Again, the image of Juliet flashed before his eyes.

Chapter Nineteen

Juliet walked into The Mistletoe pub that night with Zoe by her side. She was looking forward to seeing Dan again; they had been friends for years, but she wasn't relishing the prospect of seeing Harrison. And Zoe had told her they were meeting him and Luke in the pub, and had specifically asked her to 'be nice'.

'I'm always nice,' Juliet protested.

'Not to Harrison, you're not.'

Juliet promised she would be nothing but sweet, polite and friendly. But as she stepped inside the door, one look at Harrison's back as he stood at the bar, and she wasn't sure she could go any further, let alone pretend to be pleased to see him.

The trouble was, merely looking at his back sent shivers of excitement running through her. What would she be like when he turned around and smiled? Assuming he did smile. She quickly scanned the pub but could see no sign of Kiki. Perhaps the woman was in the loo.

'Zoe!' Luke was clearly happy to see Zoe. 'And Juliet. Hi.'

Harrison turned around but Juliet didn't get a chance to see his face. From out of nowhere a tall, blond, athletic man slammed into her, lifted her off the ground and spun her around in circles.

'Juliet! My darling, Juliet. You have no idea how happy I am to see you.'

In spite of the surprise, she laughed, realising who it was. 'And I'm happy to see you, Dan. Now please put me down before I feel sick.'

He let her feet slide to the floor but kept his arms wrapped tightly around her as he planted a kiss on her cheek.

'Paula tells me you almost died. Is that true, my darling?'

She glanced in Harrison's direction but he was no longer standing where he had been.

'Um. Yes, it's true. Harrison saved me.'

'Thank God for that. What would I have done without you? My life would've been bereft of hope and happiness. Come and tell me all about it. We're having a bit of a BBQ outside. And before you say it's too cold, this is mild compared to northern Norway at the moment. Besides, there's a huge fire and chairs and lots of lovely warm throws to wrap around us. And you can always cuddle up to me to keep warm.'

158

With his arm still wrapped around her, he led her out towards the river bank, waving with one hand to indicate that anyone who wanted to, should follow. It was only as she kissed Dan on the cheek and wiped off her lipstick mark with her finger that she saw Harrison scowling at her. What on earth had annoyed him?

'Come on, Zoe,' Dan said, as they passed. 'And you can bring your friend Luke and that hunk of a brother of his. What's his name? Oh wait. It's Harrison. Come on Harrison. I'm sure you don't feel the cold.'

Dan smiled at them and they all smiled back. Apart from Harrison. He did follow them outside though.

It was a cold night, with no cloud cover to speak of and the stars looked like tiny ice cubes in the black expanse of sky. There was hardly any snow remaining on the ground, and only small chunks of ice left in the river, sparkling like jewels in the burbling water, beneath the glow of the rows and rows of fairy lights strung up around the garden and the river bank.

'Are you having a party?' Luke asked.

'Yes,' replied Dan. 'A homecoming party for me and Juliet.'

'You're coming home?' Juliet was astonished.

Dan nodded and grinned from ear to ear. 'Yep,' he said, and burst into the England World Cup football anthem, replacing his name and then Juliet's with the word 'football'.

'Your gran didn't mention it when I saw her the day I arrived.'

'That's because she didn't know. No one knew.' He leant closer and whispered so that only Juliet could hear. 'I've met someone and I'm in love. I'll tell you all about it later.'

Juliet turned to face him and threw her arms around his neck. 'Oh Dan. I'm so happy. That's the best news I've had for ages. Oh. Apart from the fact that Zoe's in love with Luke.'

'Really?' Dan looked surprised. 'Luke Bow? This Luke?'

'The very same,' said Luke, smiling across at him, in spite of Dan's evident surprise.

'Well, let me congratulate you both,' Dan said, letting go of Juliet and hugging Luke and Zoe heartily. 'There's nothing as wonderful as being in love, is there?' He pulled Juliet back into his arms and gave her another massive hug.

'No, Dan. There isn't.' She smiled up into his eyes.

She was so pleased for him. Being gay had been a huge struggle for Dan and he still hadn't officially told his family. Juliet had known for ages but had been sworn to secrecy. No one else knew. Dan's family still hoped there might be a future together for him and Juliet. Particularly his gran, Mrs D. Juliet had urged him, over the years, to tell them. After all, being gay was no big deal. The Dobbies were lovely people and she was sure they'd be happy for him. But Dan had experienced some pretty awful bullying in his younger days and he wasn't yet prepared to let his guard down completely.

But now Dan was in love. Surely that meant he would finally tell his family? She'd have a long talk with him later when they could grab some time alone.

'Marshmallows,' Dan said, easing Juliet away from him. 'We need to toast some marshmallows over this glorious fire. And some chestnuts. And some of those delightful little cocktail sausages. I'll go and see what else Paula's got ferreted away. I know there're chicken wings, and big, fat, meaty burgers. Back in a jiffy, darling. Save me a seat by the fire.' He kissed her on the cheek once more and dashed back inside the pub.

Juliet looked around at the fairy lights as the flames from the fire reached high into the cold night air. Chairs had been placed in a wide circle around the large firepit, with cushions and throws scattered, or piled here and there. There were a couple of waterproofed-backed picnic rugs on the ground, also strewn with cushions and throws, and Christmas music wafted towards them from inside the pub.

'So that's Daniel Dobbie.' Harrison's voice made her jump.

'Yes. That's Dan. He's lovely.'

'So it seems. You look a lot happier than you did the last time I saw you.'

Juliet's cheeks burned, but it wasn't from the fire. Why did he have to smell so good? Scents of sandalwood and vanilla filled her nostrils as he stood by her side. And why did he have to look so bloody gorgeous? Even frowning, he was sexy. Simply looking at him made her heart thump in her chest and her stomach do somersaults.

'Do I? I suppose I am. I'm fully recovered from my brush with death. Thanks to you. And I discovered that my little sister is in love. Who wouldn't be happy?'

He shrugged. 'And she's not the only one, is she?'

Juliet smiled. 'No. Luke's in love too.'

'I wasn't referring to Luke.'

'Oh?'

What did that mean? Was he telling her he was also in love? With the drop-dead gorgeous Kiki, obviously.

'I wish you well,' he said, giving her a very strange look. And then he walked away to talk to the Reverend Noah Waters, Dan's great-uncle, who was at least seventy, but looked more like fifty in his jeans, crew-necked sweater and trendy, leather biker-jacket.

'It's chilly out here, dear.' Mrs D came and gave Juliet a hug. 'It won't be long before I'm back inside, mark my words. But then this is really for the youngsters, isn't it?' She nodded towards the fire and the fairy lights. 'What wouldn't I give to be your age, dear Juliet. Daniel looked mighty pleased to see you. Any chance there'll be news of another romance before too long?'

Juliet smiled. 'If there is, it won't involve me.'

Mrs D sighed. 'But how are you feeling, my dear? To think we almost lost you. Extraordinarily brave of young Harrison to jump in after you and save your life.'

'Yes. Incredibly so. In fact, I don't think I've thanked him properly. But what do you say to someone who's risked their life to save your own, apart from thank you?'

Mrs D looked thoughtful. 'I don't know, dear. But it's coming up to Christmas. You could buy him a little gift. I know the man has more money than the rest of us put together, but there must be something he wants. Possibly something money can't buy?'

'Like what?'

'No point in asking me, dear. I hardly know the man. But there must be someone who knows him well enough to know exactly what he wants. Ask Luke.'

'I think Kiki knows exactly what he wants. But I can't buy that.'

'What's that dear? And who's Kiki?'

'She's Harrison's girlfriend.'

Mrs D raised her brows and her mouth fell open for a second before a smile spread across her lips. 'Is she indeed? He certainly kept that quiet. Daphne never mentioned him having a girlfriend.

She did say he was bringing his executive assistant with him for Christmas and was hoping to get a lot of work done while he was here. She didn't say anything about a girlfriend though. My, my. I'll have to have a word with her tomorrow and catch up on all the latest gossip. Or perhaps I can get it directly from the horse's mouth. I need to have a word with my brother in any case. Excuse me, dear, while I go and talk to Noah. Make sure you have fun. And don't forget, we'd be more than happy to welcome you to the Dobbie family. You and Daniel look so good together.'

Juliet watched her shuffle away towards the Reverend and Harrison. What would Mrs D say when Dan told her the truth? Would she finally stop trying to pair them up? But at least Mrs D had given her an idea. She could buy Harrison a present as a way of saying thank you. She had no intention of asking Kiki what to buy, but Luke would know. She would ask him later, and tomorrow she, Zoe and their mum would go into town to do their final Christmas present shopping.

It wasn't long before Dan reappeared, laden down with plates and sealed containers of food. He even had a bag of marshmallows hanging from his teeth.

Juliet laughed. 'Need a hand?'

Dan merely nodded. She took the bag of marshmallows and some of the containers and set them on a table near the fire. There wasn't much space left once Dan had unburdened himself of the rest.

'Good grief,' he said. 'I feel like a donkey. But where would I find one at this time of night?' He laughed at his own joke.

'How many people are you expecting? There's enough food here for the entire weekend.'

'That's just for you, darling. I know how much you like to eat.'

'Excuse me. But you're the one who devoured an entire tin of Quality Street last Christmas. And washed that down with two plates of chilli.'

'What can I say? I'm a strapping young man.' He grinned at her and then came and stood in front of her and pulled a rather odd face. 'Don't look now, darling, but Harrison is giving us some awfully peculiar looks. Has been since the moment you arrived, I believe. Now I have to say, if I wasn't in love, I might make a play for him myself, but I am, so I won't. The thing is, darling. I'm not sure it's me he's looking at.'

Juliet glanced in Harrison's direction. Dan was right. He was looking directly at them, appearing to ignore what Noah and Mrs D were saying, and there was such a scowl on his face that he looked as if he were ready to kill someone.

'Whoever it is he's looking at, it's a pretty murderous look. I don't think I've done anything to incur his wrath tonight. In fact, a moment ago, he wished me well.'

Dan threw a hasty look at Harrison over his shoulder and quickly returned his gaze to Juliet. 'Are you ill?'

'No. I'm perfectly fine.'

'Then why did he wish you well?'

Juliet tutted. 'I think … Actually, I have no idea. I assumed he meant he hoped I had a good evening.'

'Then he would have said, "Have a good evening," wouldn't he?'

'I suppose so. Oh wait. Kiki's still not here. That explains it. He's had a row with his girlfriend and he's simply in a bad mood.'

'What? And he's annoyed that everyone else is having a good time?'

'Yes.'

'Then why isn't he looking at everyone else?' Dan darted another look over his shoulder. 'Nope. Definitely us. You know what? I think we should just ignore him, darling. No. I think we should have even more fun until he's so cross, he's fit to burst.'

'Why?'

'Because I simply don't like the way he's looking at us. The man needs to lighten up.' He grabbed Juliet's hand and pulled her into his arms. 'Come along, darling. Let's dance.'

Dan whirled her around like a professional ballroom dancer, even on the uneven ground, and he expertly avoided all the icy patches. Each time she whizzed past Harrison's face it grew angrier. He was evidently in a terrible mood.

Juliet was having fun, but she needed to catch her breath. She'd been dancing and laughing; spun around so many times that she was having trouble staying upright. She longed to sit for ten minutes or so and eventually she told Dan she needed to go and sit on one of the chairs close to the fire. Reluctantly, he let her go.

She wanted to simply enjoy the warmth, the lights and the starlit sky. The moon was bright again tonight; tomorrow it would be full and as she stared up at it she emptied her mind of thought, save for how beautiful it was. She didn't even notice Harrison come and sit beside her, until he said her name.

Her hand flew to her heart. 'Dear God, Harrison. You made me jump. I was miles away.'

'I'm beginning to wish I was. I wish I hadn't come back.'

'Feeling sorry for yourself? But why?' A thought struck her and she bridled, sitting upright. She gave him a cool stare. 'Is this about Zoe and your brother? I didn't expect you to be happy about it but wishing you weren't here is a bit much, isn't it?'

'Whoa! Where did that come from? It's got nothing to do with Zoe and Luke. I couldn't be happier for him. For both of them. You can see how much they love one another just by looking at them.'

He nodded his head in the direction the two were standing. They were staring up at the moon, just as Juliet had been, but they were arm in arm with their heads touching, and were so close together it was hard to see where Zoe ended and Luke began.

'Yes. But they hid it well. I had no idea until she told me on Wednesday.'

He shook his head. 'Nor did I. I didn't even know he was seeing anyone. I guess that makes me a bad brother.'

'If it does, then I'm an equally bad sister. I didn't know Zoe had a boyfriend, either. But it's amazing how people can keep their relationship quiet, if they want to, isn't it?'

'You can say that again.'

She gave him a sideways glance. 'So why are you wishing you hadn't come back? I'd have drowned, if you hadn't.'

'That's true. I'm glad I was there for that.'

'And I don't think I've thanked you properly. You were brave and kind and I didn't really show my appreciation.'

'There's no need. I'm just glad you're safe.'

'You still haven't said why you wish you weren't here.'

He twisted his pint glass between his fingers. 'Too many memories. And not much to look forward to.'

She watched him for a moment but he didn't look up from his glass.

'The memories bit I understand. But as to not having much to look forward to, I don't get that at all. Apart from the fact that you've probably got enough money to go anywhere you want, whenever you want, you've got everything to look forward to. You're helping Luke and Zoe get their business off the ground, so Zoe tells me. That's really kind, and definitely something to excite you, I would've thought. And once Luke actually proposes, there'll be an engagement party, a wedding, and who knows what after that.'

'That's the part that worries me.'

'What? Them having children?'

His head shot round and he met her eyes. 'No.' He shook his head. 'Having to come back here for all of it.'

She sucked in an angry breath. 'Do you hate it here that much?'

He shrugged and shook his head once more.

'Well, tough. Not everything's about you, Harrison.' She stopped and bit her lip. 'Sorry. I promised Zoe I'd be nice.'

His eyes narrowed and his fingers tightened on the glass. 'You did what? Zoe told you to be *nice* to me? That's just great. That's perfect. So if she hadn't, you'd have ignored me again, would you? Or walked away as you love to do.'

'No. That didn't come out right. You just …'

'I just what?'

'Oh, I don't know. You just make me really angry sometimes, Harrison.'

'Ditto.'

'I make you angry? Why? What have I done?'

'Oh, I don't know,' he imitated her to a T. 'How about flaunting your boyfriend in front of me, for one thing.'

'My boyfriend? You've got a bloody nerve. Especially after you flaunted your girlfriend in front of me.'

'What *are* you talking about?'

'I'm talking about sending her to my room, straight from having sex with you in the shower, on the pretence of getting her to "see if I was okay". The woman was virtually naked. Now that's what I call flaunting.'

'What woman? When?'

'The most beautiful woman in the world, of course. To my bedroom at The Grange. After you saved my life.'

His brows furrowed. 'You must've been delusional. That can happen after hypothermia. I told you, you needed to take care. I didn't send anyone to your room. Not before, or after having sex in the shower. No. What I mean is, I wasn't having sex in the shower – or anywhere else for that matter – with anyone, let alone the most beautiful woman in the world. What exactly did she look like?'

'Delusional? That's your response is it? So you deny sending her to my room in the flimsiest, shortest dressing gown, ever, do you? And rubbing my nose in it. Let's ask Kiki, shall we? Where is she, anyway? Have you two had a row? Is that why you're behaving like a bear with a sore head?'

'Kiki? What the hell's Kiki got to do with anything? And no, we haven't had a row. Just a little misunderstanding, that's all.'

'Well, I hope you sort it, Harrison, because getting cross with other people simply because they're having a good time and you're not, is frankly, pretty childish.'

'Julie-et?' Dan intervened before Harrison could make any response; if indeed he was going to. 'Come and help me toast the marshmallows, darling. You're so much better at this sort of thing.' He grabbed her hand and pulled her away and as she turned her head briefly to look back, Harrison stormed off towards the road.

Chapter Twenty

It must have started snowing in the middle of the night because when Juliet pulled back her curtains at seven-thirty on Saturday morning, there was at least six inches of pristine snow, for as far as the eye could see.

She threw on her dressing gown over her favourite pyjamas – Christmas Unicorns in Santa Hats – and went downstairs to the kitchen, where a choir from one or other cathedral boomed out Christmas carols via the radio.

'Morning.' Only her mum was in the kitchen, leaning over the stove stirring a saucepan of porridge. Rosa still made it the old-fashioned way.

'Morning, sweetheart. Did you have a good time last night? Your father and I were tucked up in bed when you and Zoe came home, so I assume it was fun.'

'Yeah. It was great. Dan was on top form and he'd organised a sort of BBQ. We all sat outside under the stars, kept warm by a massive fire pit. I wouldn't be surprised if it's still burning this morning.'

She poured herself coffee from the pot, and popped several slices of bread in the toaster, trying not to trip over Cinnamon who, as usual, was sprawled between the Aga and the kitchen table.

'It'll be buried under all this snow,' Rosa said. 'Shopping's going to be a bit of an expedition in this weather. Still, there's nothing quite as Christmassy as shopping for presents, trudging through snow. We'll need to make a day of it. Perhaps we'll go somewhere nice for lunch. We'll see what your father and Zoe have to say.'

'That would be nice.' Juliet threw her a sideways glance as she pulled out a chair and sat at the table. 'Mum? May I ask for some advice?'

'Of course, sweetheart. What is it?' Rosa took the saucepan off the stove and put it to one side, before pouring herself a coffee and sitting next to Juliet.

'Do you think I should buy Harrison a present? Not a Christmas present, exactly, but something to say thanks for saving me and for letting me spend the night at The Grange.'

'I think that's a lovely idea. What are you thinking of getting him? Men are always difficult to buy for, especially men like Harrison who has everything he could possibly need or want.'

'That's the problem. I don't know what to get him, but I want to get him something. I asked Luke if he had any ideas, but he said he can't think of a thing Harrison doesn't already have. At least, nothing that money can buy.'

'That was an odd thing to say.'

Juliet had said that about Kiki, but she nodded. 'Yeah. Not much help, either. I'll have to have a look around in town and see if anything jumps out at me.'

The ping of the toaster announced the toast was ready just as Zoe and Bernard ambled into the kitchen.

'I suggested we spend the day in town, darling,' Rosa said, as Bernard gave her a kiss. 'Not just the morning. We'll have lunch and then come back and have a light supper this evening. How does that sound?'

'Perfect,' Bernard said, kissing Juliet on the top of her head and taking his seat at the table.

Zoe squealed and jumped up and down, waving her phone in her hand.

'Zoe thinks it's a good plan,' said Juliet, pulling a face at her sister.

'What? Oh I wasn't getting excited about shopping and lunch. I was getting excited about this. Look!'

Zoe passed her phone in front of them but it was so fast Juliet didn't see a thing.

'I didn't see it. What was it?'

'It's an invitation to dinner tonight.'

'Lovely. Oh! From Luke? Does this mean he's going to propose tonight?'

Zoe frowned. 'What? No. I mean yes, it's from Luke, but it's not for me. Well not just for me. It's for us. For all of us. We've been invited to dinner at The Grange tonight. Luke says he knows it's short notice but it would mean a lot if we could come.' She looked at each of them in turn, her smile fading slightly. 'We will go, won't we? All of us.' She stared at Juliet.

'Hey. Don't look at me like that. It is short notice. Very short notice and I think it's a bit of a cheek, but of course I'll go if it'll make you happy. Even though I'd rather throw myself back in the lake and drown than have dinner at The Grange.'

Even Bernard stiffened. 'I agree with Juliet. It's very short notice, especially in this weather, and so close to Christmas Day.' He glanced at Rosa before smiling at Zoe. 'But if you and Luke are going to be spending your future together, I suppose we'll all have to get used to passing an evening or two at the house.'

Rosa smiled wanly. 'Does he say if it's a formal affair, sweetheart? Or casual?'

'Oh. He doesn't say. I'll send him a text and ask.'

Juliet tutted. 'Why don't you call him? That way we can ask what time it is. Who'll be there? How long it's likely to last. Can I bring a plus one? Because I'm not looking forward to Harrison and Kiki pawing one another in front of me while I sit there twiddling my thumbs.'

175

Zoe smirked. 'Forgetting for one moment that you don't have a plus one you can take, why would Harrison and Kiki be pawing one another?'

'They might not be I suppose, if they're still having their little misunderstanding.'

'What misunderstanding?'

'I don't know. I didn't ask the details. But they must've had a row because she wasn't there last night and Harrison was biting everyone's heads off. He was in such a bad mood. I suppose they could've made up last night though because he left ten minutes after he arrived. Well maybe not ten minutes, but he certainly didn't hang around.'

Zoe chuckled and shook her head. 'I don't know what you're talking about. But I'll ask.' She went into the hall and closed the kitchen door behind her.

'I'm not looking forward to this, darling,' Bernard said, casting a melancholy look at Rosa.

'Nor am I,' she replied. 'I'm not sure why we need to go to dinner. He hasn't proposed yet.'

'Perhaps Rufus wants to make it clear the past is in the past.'

'Oh God,' Juliet said. 'Will he be there?'

Rosa raised her brows. 'I should think so sweetheart. It is his house, after all.'

'Oh joy. I'm not sure I've got anything to wear. Especially not if it's a formal affair.'

'Then it's probably a good thing we're going shopping. You can pick up something in town.'

'Great. I've got to buy a dress to go to a dinner I don't want to go to with people I don't like. Present company excepted.' She shook her head and reached out her hand to her dad. 'Will it be awful for you, Dad? I know you got through having to come and see me the other day, but this is different. We've got to go to the house that was our home and sit and watch as that old man lords it over us.'

'He might not do that,' Rosa said, as Juliet got up to grab some toast. 'Harrison was nothing but kind when we were there, and he made sure I had everything I needed to make me feel comfortable. I don't see why Rufus would go out of his way to make us feel uneasy or unwelcome. Not after so many years. At least I hope he won't.'

Zoe shoved open the door, all smiles. 'Okay. Dinner's at eight. Luke will come and get us. Casual not formal. No need for you to dress up. What else? Um. He'll bring us home whenever we want. It'll just be them and us. No one else is invited. Um. And no, you can't take anyone with you, Juliet. Right. I think that covers it. God, I'm starving. What time are we going shopping? I need to buy a new dress.'

Juliet's jaw dropped as she returned to the table with a plate of toast. 'I thought you said it was casual and we didn't need to dress up.'

Zoe grabbed a slice from Juliet's plate and grinned. 'I said *you* didn't need to dress up. I intend to knock both Luke and the old man, dead.

Figuratively speaking, of course. I don't want old Rufus to die the first time I go to dinner with him. And I definitely don't want Luke to kick the bucket. At least not before he's proposed. Sorry! I shouldn't joke about that, should I? Not after what happened to you, sis.'

But Juliet wasn't thinking about that. If Zoe was going to buy a new dress in the hope of knocking her boyfriend's socks off, so to speak, then perhaps Juliet should do the same. Buy a new dress and see if she could knock a certain person's socks off.

Although with Kiki as her competition, it would have to be one hell of a dress.

Chapter Twenty-One

Despite having spent the entire day Christmas shopping, trudging through shin-deep snow, laden down with bags and battling hordes of determined shoppers, while being brain washed into feeling jolly by the endless stream of cheery Christmas music blaring from every shop, Juliet was ready by seven-thirty and was staring out of her bedroom window towards The Grange.

When they lived there, the entire outline of house could be seen from anywhere on Mistletoe Row at this time of year; lights hung all around the façade, the roof, the windows and the door. There was a huge Christmas tree, or two, outside, with hundreds and hundreds of coloured lights swaying in the wind. A warm amber glow from the interior flooded out onto the gravel drive, making the house look both welcoming and lived in. When you opened the heavy front doors which were surrounded by boughs of pine entwined with holly and mistletoe and where a magnificent, mistletoe, holly and red rose, wreath hung, the heady aromas of spices, brandy, and herbs and baking, drifted out into the cold night air. And when you went inside, it was as if you'd been enveloped in a warm hug. There were lights and decorations adorning the tree in the hall, another in the sitting room and one in the dining room. Boughs of holly and mistletoe wound their way around each door frame. Cards and presents were everywhere. The place oozed Christmas spirit in every sense of the word.

Peering out into the darkness, Juliet could just make out the light in the hall, and one in the dining room. Harrison and Luke, along with Kiki, had been at Merry's Christmas Tree Farm on Monday, so they must've got a tree. It wasn't outside, so it must be indoors. Perhaps they got more than one. She hadn't seen any when she was there, but she had stayed in her room. She hadn't spotted one as she left on Wednesday. Did they get one, after all?

From her room, the house looked sad and lonely. It really needed cheering up. It was odd that Luke hadn't done that. But perhaps he would if Zoe mentioned it. She saw car headlights moving down the drive. Luke was on his way. She went downstairs just as Zoe called her name and a few seconds later, Luke pulled up outside.

'Sorry this was all so last minute,' he said, holding the door open for Rosa, Juliet and Zoe to get into the back, while Bernard walked around and got in the front passenger seat. 'Harrison thought it was time we all got together. Now that it's out in the open.' He slid into the front seat and smiled. 'And I apologise if you feel that Zoe and I have been running around behind your backs Mr and Mrs Bell, but the truth is, we weren't sure how you'd all feel about us seeing one another. No point in tipping up the apple cart for a few dates. Once we realised how serious we were, we knew we had to come clean, so to speak. But I wanted to wait until I could talk to Harrison. And he's been difficult to pin down.'

'We understand,' Bernard said. 'And, if we're going to be family, please call us Rosa and Bernard.'

'Thanks.' Luke put his foot on the accelerator and tore away at close to breakneck speed, sending waves of snow into the air.

Bernard coughed. 'Perhaps we could slow down. I can't see the road under all this snow.'

'I've got snow tyres and it won't matter if we venture a little off-piste.' Luke threw Bernard a confident smile, which clearly wasn't returned. 'No. You're right, of course.' Luke immediately slowed down, but it still took less than three minutes from door to door.

Juliet was surprised to see the front door open the second they arrived, and even more so, to see Harrison waiting to greet them.

'Welcome,' he said, as they got out of the car. 'Glad to see you arrived safely.'

'We didn't have far to come,' Bernard said. 'Good evening, Harrison. Good to see you again.'

'No. But …' His voice trailed off as his gaze landed on Juliet. He was probably going to comment on Luke's driving, but clearly thought better of it. 'Um. It's good to see you again too, Bernard. It's good to see you all. Please come in.'

He stood to one side to let them pass and as Juliet drew level with him, he half-smiled, half-frowned; a sort of grimacing smile, if she could call it that.

'You look beautiful, Juliet.'

His words surprised her. She knew the midnight-blue dress, which clung to her body in all the right places, but somehow managed to hide the few lumps and bumps eating too much junk food had caused, suited her. Her family had even said she looked lovely, Zoe going as far as to say, "Wowser! And I thought I would knock them dead," but Juliet had her heavy overcoat buttoned up tight, so he couldn't see it at the moment. He was clearly trying to be polite.

'Thanks. You look good too.' And he did. Charcoal grey trousers, a white shirt and a navy-blue sweater might look boring on most men; somehow Harrison made them look hot.

She glanced around the hall, met her mum's eyes and nodded. She could read her thoughts because Juliet was thinking the same.

'You look a little disappointed,' Harrison said, as he asked to take their coats and Daphne joined them from the direction of the kitchen.

'No. I was merely wondering if you bought a tree the other day, and if so, where it is, that's all.'

'In the sitting room. Daphne decorated it, with a little help from Luke so it …' He stopped mid-sentence as Juliet shrugged off her coat and handed it to him. His jaw dropped, his eyes opened wide and he blinked several times.

'What's wrong?' She looked down at her dress. It was an off-the-shoulder, scooped neck, which came to a low-cut V at the top of her breast-bone and for a second, she thought it might be revealing much more than it should. She laid a hand upon her chest and let out a soft sigh of relief. 'Phew. I thought my dress may've slipped. Um. Why are you staring at me? It's making me feel a little uncomfortable.'

He blinked again. 'You should be in my shoes. I'm stunned. You look … sensational.' He gave his head a quick shake. 'Sorry. Um. Let me take your coat, Rosa.'

He reached out his hand to take it, but his gaze was still fixed on Juliet and she could feel a rush of colour creep across her chest and up into her cheeks. A tiny smile formed on her lips. Was he actually having trouble taking his eyes off her? Did he honestly think she looked sensational? She was so pleased she'd bought this dress, even if it had cost far more than she should've spent.

'Drinks in the sitting room?' Daphne said, glancing at Harrison, as if for approval. 'Rufus is in there waiting.'

'Great,' Harrison said, but he didn't sound happy. 'Yes. Please make yourselves at home while I hang up your coats.'

'I'll do that. You go with your guests.' Daphne grabbed the coats from him and gave him an odd look, as if she was telling him that's what he should do.

'Come on,' said Luke, smiling as he took Zoe's hand and tipped his head towards the sitting room door. 'You know the way.'

They followed him to the sitting room and as he opened the door, a kaleidoscope of coloured light streamed into the hall. A majestic tree stood to one side of the room, covered in white twinkling lights and glistening multi-coloured baubles with piles of presents wrapped in gleaming paper strewn around its base. A splendid fire crackled and roared in the hearth and deep green boughs of holly and mistletoe lay along the length of the ornate marble mantlepiece, the red and white berries of each plant, looking fresh and plump and as if they were still sprinkled with frost.

It wasn't as festive as it had been when Juliet and her family lived there, but at least Harrison, Luke and Daphne had gone to some effort to make the house look Christmassy. It even looked welcoming. But Rufus didn't. He got to his feet and glared at them.

'Welcome,' he said, the tiniest hint of a smile tugging at his lips. 'I bet you never thought to be back in this room again, did you?'

'Grandfather.' Harrison's tone was quiet, but authoritative. 'I'll pour the drinks. Please sit down everyone.'

'Yeah, sit down,' Luke said, staring appreciatively at Zoe's dress, as they stood arm in arm by the tree.

'Good evening, Rufus,' Bernard said, nodding at the old man, who merely grunted in reply.

'Merry Christmas to you, Rufus.' Rosa smiled at him and his features softened a fraction.

'Hmm. Yes. Merry Christmas. Still a couple of days away though.'

Rosa's smile widened. 'Yes. But we believe in starting Christmas early. The festive season began in our house the minute Juliet came home.'

'Hmm. Where is the girl?'

Juliet, who had been trying to blend into the wall farthest from Rufus, stepped forward. She took a deep breath and held her head high.

'I'm here. Good evening Mr Bow. I hope you're well.'

His brows shot up, his eyes scanned her from head to toe and he let out a whistle before he shot a look at Harrison, who seemed to be watching Rufus with an expression on his face like a tiger ready to pounce.

To Juliet's astonishment, the old man chuckled. 'I bet you hoped I wasn't. But I don't blame you, girl.'

'Her name is Juliet,' Harrison said, with ice in his voice.

Rufus shot another look at Harrison, before chuckling again. 'Yes, yes. I know. Well, well, Juliet. You've grown into quite the stunner, haven't you?'

This time it was Juliet who shot a look at Harrison and he momentarily met her eyes.

'Have I?' She dragged her gaze back to the old man. 'Thank you, Mr Bow.'

'I suppose you should call me Rufus. Sit. I'm too old to stand around.' He dropped back into his chair but kept his eyes on Juliet.

'You're back here to live, I hear.'

'Yes.' Juliet sat as far from him as possible.

He glanced at Harrison. 'My grandson's considering the same.'

'What would you all like to drink?' Harrison hurriedly asked, giving Rufus what looked like a warning glare.

'Sherry, if you have it, please,' Rosa said.

'I'll get ours,' said Luke, finally moving away from Zoe and walking over to Harrison.

'Same for me, please,' said Bernard.

'Zoe'll have a G&T,' Luke said.

'Juliet?' Harrison gave her an odd smile.

'Same for me. G&T that is, please.'

The sitting room door burst open and Kiki sauntered in. Her red dress was like a second skin, so tight you could see her hip bones. And that wasn't all you could see. She clearly wasn't wearing a bra. Juliet sucked in her breath and glanced at Harrison from beneath her lashes. He turned, gave a half-hearted smile and went back to pouring the drinks.

Had the man gone blind? Or had he seen Kiki's body so many times that it no longer had any effect on him?

'Kiki!' Rufus jumped to his feet like a man half his age and reached out a gnarled hand. 'Come and sit by me, my dear. You put the fire to shame. I thought Juliet here might've outshone you tonight, but not by half.'

Kiki darted a look at Juliet, her eyes narrowing for a split second, her mouth forming a tight line before being hastily replaced by a smile.

'Hello, Juliet. So lovely to see you again. And in such a pretty dress. I hope that didn't blow your budget. And all your family, too. Hello Zoe. You're looking lovely. And Rosa. We met briefly when you stayed the other day. Nice to see you again. And this handsome devil must be Bernard. I didn't get a chance to say hello when you were here last time. How does it feel to be a dinner guest in what was once your home?'

'Kiki.' Harrison's voice was cold.

'Yes, Harrison?'

Their gaze held and the room fell silent for a milli-second, but it felt like longer as Juliet watched the expression on Harrison's face. It went from angry to calm in a moment.

'What would you like to drink?'

'The usual,' she said, with the coolest of smiles, before sashaying over to Rufus and sitting on the chair beside him, her arm draped casually on the arm of his.

Kiki had clearly got into Rufus' good books. The old man couldn't take his eyes from her. Juliet felt a twinge of envy. She didn't like Rufus but he was Harrison's grandfather. Perhaps they were also putting the past behind them; obviously with a little help from Kiki.

Conversation was stilted for the first few minutes, but eventually, as Harrison said how pleased he was that Luke had been sensible enough to fall in love with Zoe and how sure he was that they had a bright and extremely happy future together, the tension vanished.

'Only if he actually proposes,' Zoe joked.

'Ah yes. About that. Luke placed his glass on the side table, took Zoe's left hand in his and got down on one knee, taking a small, plush velvet box from his trouser pocket. 'Zoe Rosa Bell, I know you could probably do better than a man like me, who often has his head in the clouds, and didn't have a clue where he was going, until he met you. But you're my heaven. My future. You made me stop daydreaming and helped me turn my hopes and desires into reality. I love you with all my heart. Will you make my last outstanding dream come true and say you'll be my wife?' He opened the lid and the ring inside sparkled brighter than all the lights on the tree beside him.

'Yes,' Zoe said, tears of delight filling her eyes. 'Oh yes, Luke. And I couldn't do better than you. You're the best man in the world.'

He slid the ring on her finger, got to his feet and pulled her into his arms and kissed her as everyone clapped and cheered. Even Rufus smiled and nodded.

Juliet glanced at Harrison and had to gasp for breath. He was looking directly at her and the look in his eyes was unmistakable.

A look she hadn't seen for twenty years.

No one but Harrison had ever looked at her like that, nor made her feel that way.

It was as if he was in agony and ecstasy at one and the same time.

And as if they were floating in the universe with nothing around them except exploding stars and careering planets.

At least it seemed that way to her.

A sudden flash before her eyes made her blink, and then she saw that Zoe was holding out her hand, a circle of diamonds around a blood red ruby glinting on her finger.

'Isn't it the most gorgeous ring you've ever seen?' Zoe asked, her voice as high as the ceiling.

'It is,' Juliet replied. 'Congratulations.' She hugged Zoe to her and seconds later, when she glanced across to where Harrison had been standing, he had gone to congratulate Luke.

Chapter Twenty-Two

What a strange evening it had been? Juliet had hardly slept a wink thinking about it. She'd thought about it in the shower too, and during breakfast when they'd all discussed the events of the night – but not about what passed between her and Harrison. Only she seemed aware of that. Was it possible she had imagined it?

Perhaps it had just been wishful thinking, brought on by Luke proposing to Zoe. Maybe it was because she had longed for Harrison to look at her in the way Luke was looking at her sister, so in her confused brain, he had. After all, it had only been for those few seconds. During dinner, he had hardly glanced in her direction. Even when he talked to her, from way down the table, his eyes seemed to look at everyone and everything but her. And when she and her family had left, several hours later, it had been Daphne who had handed them their coats, and Luke who had driven them home. Harrison had merely said a brief good night and had disappeared into his study.

Perhaps she had annoyed him by reminiscing; by telling Luke what Christmas had been like when her family lived at The Grange. But Luke had asked, and so had Harrison, now she came to think about it. And all she'd really said was that all their guests could've seen the house from miles away because there had been so many trees and lights and decorations. And she'd only mentioned the drinks party on Christmas Eve for everyone who lived on Mistletoe Row, in passing. It wasn't her fault Luke had said how depressingly miserable the house must seem to her and her family now. Okay, maybe she shouldn't have said it did. But at least she was being honest. Surely that was a good thing?

She was still thinking about how strange it had been as she and her family walked along Mistletoe Row, ankle deep in snow, to go to church. In fact, everything had been strange since she'd come home. It was even odd that they were all going to church. They never went to church. But Zoe had insisted.

'You know what the Reverend's like,' Zoe had said over breakfast. 'He may be trendy in the way he acts and dresses, but as far as the church goes, he's living back in the fourteenth century, when the church still reigned over 'peasants' like us. If we don't show our faces for the next few weeks, there's no way he'll agree to marry me and

Luke. And all my life I've dreamt of getting married in St Clement's, so we're going and that means all of us.'

'You've got mighty bossy since last night,' Juliet joked. 'Just because you're marrying someone from the Big House, it doesn't mean you can expect us to bow and curtsy to you.'

Zoe laughed. 'I can't imagine you bowing and curtsying to anyone and I don't recall anyone doing that to us when we lived there. It is a bit weird though, isn't it? I mean, actually being invited to go up there whenever I feel like it, instead of merely staring at it from our door.'

Rosa and Bernard had said that it was definitely a little strange to be told that they should consider the place a second home, bearing in mind it had actually been their first home and that of the Bell family, for hundreds of years before.

As they had left their cottage, they had all glanced up at The Grange, still looking rather forlorn, and possibly more so on such a cloudy morning, when the sky seemed about to burst from the weight of snow waiting to fall.

'Yep. It's definitely weird knowing I can go there without being turned away at the door,' Zoe said.

'And not just you, sweetheart.' Rosa stepped over a large mound of snow that must've fallen from their roof. 'Harrison said we can all go up as often as we like.'

Bernard took Rosa's hand and slipped her arm through his. 'Harrison meant well. But I don't think I'll be popping in and out. Although it was civil of Rufus not to retract the invitation. It's almost as if he's letting Harrison get a feel for what it'll be like once he eventually inherits the place.'

'Will he inherit it?' Juliet asked.

'It's almost certain he will. Rufus only had one son and he died years ago, so Harrison is the next in line. Whether he'll want to live there or not is a different matter entirely.'

'I thought I heard Rufus say that Harrison was considering it,' Rosa said. 'At least that was the impression I got. That Harrison may be returning to The Grange.'

'He is,' Zoe said. 'Luke told me last night. Harrison had a long talk with him on Saturday morning and one of the things he said was that he was contemplating moving back. He also told Luke that he and I can live there if we like. He said the house is big enough for us all not to bump into one another every second of the day. Which I can confirm. He also said, if we preferred, there may be some way of converting it into separate accommodations for him and us, without altering the interior too much. Don't look so panicked, the three of you. You know it's listed, so I doubt he'd get permission. And I wouldn't want him to. Like you, I think the house should remain as it is. No reason why we shouldn't live there as a family though. At least until the business is bringing in enough for us to get a place of our own.'

Juliet felt a little envious. 'Just as well it's so big. I wouldn't fancy bumping into Kiki every five minutes if I were in your shoes.'

Zoe laughed. 'Firstly, you shouldn't be wearing my shoes. Your feet are a size bigger than mine. And secondly, Kiki won't be there, so that wouldn't be a problem. Look, there's Dan.'

Dan rushed through the snow towards them before Juliet could ask why Zoe was so sure Kiki wouldn't be living there.

'Hello all. I hear congratulations are in order. Let me see the ring.' He grabbed Zoe's hand, yanked off her glove and winked at Juliet. 'Hello darling. I've got lots to tell you. Grab me after church and I'll buy you a drink or two. Oh Zoe.' He shielded his eyes with one hand. 'It's so bright I'm blinded. How did he propose?'

Dan beamed at Rosa and Bernard before linking his arms through Zoe's and Juliet's and marching them towards the church, while Zoe told him all about the proposal and Juliet wondered if Harrison really would come back to live at The Grange. And if he did, why he wouldn't be bringing Kiki with him.

Perhaps he and Kiki had fallen out, after all. And even though Juliet knew it was a bit bitchy of her, she couldn't help but smile at that thought.

Chapter Twenty-Three

Juliet sat in a cosy corner of The Mistletoe, nursing another glass of mulled wine. She was on her first glass when Dan told her all about Louis, the man he loved. She'd nearly finished her second, when he explained how difficult it had been to get his family together yesterday due to the fact that they all worked; his Dad and step Mum at the pub, his grandparents at the store, and his great-uncle at the church. She was about to start on her third when he finally told her how they had reacted to his news.

'I started off by telling them that it was never going to happen between you and me, because when I said I had two big announcements to make and needed them to let me finish before they said one word, Gran jumped in and said, "Finally, you and Juliet are dating, aren't you?"' Dan rolled his eyes. 'Well, I said, "Sorry, Gran. That dog won't hunt. Juliet is not my type, although I love her to bits. But I have found my soulmate and that's why we're having this conversation."'

'Does that mean she'll never tease me about you and me again?'

Dan nodded. 'You can count on it, darling. So anyway, I began by telling them all about Louis. I told them how wonderful it'll be because he only lives thirty miles or so from here. I told them he's a pilot. That he's thirty-eight so only two years older than me, and that we have all the same interests in common. Then Noah says, "Shouldn't it be pronounced Louise, with an 'e' on the end?" And Dad says, "I'm confused. I thought we were talking about a man. Are we talking about a woman?" And Paula, who later said she and Dad had known all along that I was gay and that it really isn't an issue, says, "Dan's in love with his new boyfriend. And I'm sure none of us has a problem with that, do we, Noah?"' Dan shook his head and laughed. 'Because let's face it, darling, Noah would be the only one with any reservations, wouldn't he? But he didn't have any. Until I told him Louis is an atheist. Noah looked fit to burst, and said we'd have to do something about that. Can you imagine Gran's face?'

'Was she upset?'

Dan shook his head again. 'Only about the atheist bit. And that it had dawned on Paula before the rest of them, that I was gay. And then Paula piped up, "You can't force a person to believe in God if they don't want to. And if Dan's in love with an atheist, we're all going to have to get used to that, aren't we?" Oddly enough, Gran seems to like Paula more now. She asked her opinion on serving low-fat brandy butter with the Christmas pud this year instead of full fat. Thank God Paula said full fat, or she might've slid back down in Gran's estimation. It seems, my being gay and in love, has brought everyone closer together, in spite of Louis' beliefs. And when I said I hadn't told Mum or my step-dad about Louis yet, they were even more overjoyed. That was a little fib, of course. Mum was the first to know, but as she and Dad haven't spoken since I was about ten, no one here will ever find out I lied. Dad and Mum only exchange emails if they want to ask one another something about me, and my love-life is hardly a topic they'd ever discuss. Even now.'

Juliet smiled. 'All this time you've been worried about how everyone would react, and all it's done is improved Paula's relationship with your gran. You must be so happy.'

'I'm delirious, darling. In a good way of course.'

'Oh Dan!' She shrieked much louder than she'd intended. 'I'm so happy I could cry.'

Dan shrieked too. 'Oh darling, so am I.'

She threw her arms around him and they hugged for several minutes. It was only when she eased herself away to ask when she was going to be able to meet Louis, that she saw several of the customers looking at them, one of whom, was

Harrison. He was standing directly opposite, by the bar, and he definitely wasn't happy.

'Does that man ever do anything other than scowl?' Dan asked, following the direction of her gaze. 'Would it kill him to smile? I'm sure he'd look gorgeous if he did.'

Harrison turned away, said something to Paula, and disappeared via the front door of the pub.

'He's gorgeous even when he's scowling,' Juliet said, sighing deeply.

'Oh dear, darling.' Dan pulled a face. 'You've really got it bad, haven't you? I know you've had the hots for the hunk since you were sixteen but I thought you were trying to get over it. Has his being here made things worse?'

'You have no idea, Dan.' Juliet slouched against the seat. 'I've tried really hard to fight it, but it seems there's nothing I can do. I may as well join a convent. Or perhaps I should be locked up. I mean, dear God, is it normal to fall so madly in love with someone you've just met, that you stay in love with them for twenty years? Even though you think you hate them? And the worst part is, I think I'm going to love that bloody man for my entire life.'

Dan sighed. 'I don't know, darling. This is the first time I've been in love.'

Paula appeared, bearing two more glasses of mulled wine.

'Thanks, Paula,' Juliet said, 'But I'm not sure I should have any more. This'll be my fourth.'

'It's Christmas, love,' said Paula, handing Dan the other glass.

'Thanks, Mum,' Dan said, smiling and winking at her.

Paula beamed at him. 'You're very welcome, son.'

Juliet glanced from one to the other.

'Don't look so astonished, darling,' Dan said. 'It's time I also called wicked Paula, Mum and it's time she called me her son. We decided last night, over one or two Tequilas, didn't we, Mum?'

Paula nodded. 'We did indeed, son. But I'm not allowed to call him 'love' or 'darling'.' She winked at Juliet. 'You're the only one he ever calls darling.'

'Am I?'

Dan nodded. 'Yes, darling, you are. Or you were, before I met Louis. But I'll still call you darling even though I'm so deeply in love. You are my two darlings, and that will never change.'

'I'd never noticed that before,' Juliet said.

'Well, Harrison noticed,' Paula said. 'He came in here looking for you, but when I pointed in your direction, his face fell as if he had a lump of concrete attached to his chin. And what a handsome chin it is.'

Juliet blinked. 'He … he was looking for me?''

'Yep. But he said it didn't matter because he'd already told your mum, and he left. Oh, but he did invite us all to drinks up at The Grange on Christmas Eve. He says he's inviting everyone who lives on Mistletoe Row. And even though that's tomorrow, and one of our busiest nights of the year, Kevin and I'll get the staff to cover for us for an hour or two. I'm not going to miss a chance to poke around The Grange. Not for all the beer in our barrels.'

'Wow!' Dan said. 'And if he's inviting everyone on the street, most of your punters will be up there at some stage during the evening. I'm definitely going. Although it would've been nice if he'd invited us in person, wouldn't it, darling.' He nudged Juliet's arm 'We were only a few metres away from the grump, for heaven's sake.'

'Drinks on Christmas Eve?' Juliet repeated, bemused. 'At The Grange?'

'Yep. Are you feeling okay, love? Perhaps you're right. Perhaps you have had enough mulled wine.'

'Not nearly enough, Paula,' Juliet said, grabbing the glass and knocking back the contents in one long gulp, even though it was warmer than she remembered and she burnt her tongue.

Chapter Twenty-Four

What was Harrison playing at? Drinks on Christmas Eve? Juliet kicked up piles of snow as she trudged back to the cottage. And Dan was right. Why didn't Harrison come over and invite her and Dan face-to-face? Especially as he'd told Paula he was looking for her. And why *had* he been looking for her? She picked up speed. What had he said to her mum? She ran to the cottage and dashed inside, the smell of roast beef wafting towards her nose.

'There you are, sweetheart,' Rosa said, as Juliet burst into the kitchen. 'Harrison was here about thirty minutes ago. He's invited us to drinks tomorrow night.'

'So I heard. Did he say anything else?'

Bernard glanced up from his newspaper. 'Like what, sweetheart?'

'I don't know. But he came into the pub and Paula said he was looking for me. Did he ask you where I was?'

'Yeah', said Zoe, pointing at her magazine. 'What d'you think of this dress? It's incredibly expensive, but Luke did say I can spend as much as I like, and he'll pay. Or Harrison will. I forget which. Anyway, the point is money isn't an issue. And don't get all defensive, Dad. Luke and I agreed that we would pay for our own wedding. They cost an arm and a leg these days and neither of us want you and Mum using your savings to pay for one day.'

Rosa tutted. 'What do you think our savings are for, sweetheart?'

'I know what they should be for. They should be for you and Dad to go on a cruise or something. Neither of you has had a holiday in years.'

'We've had lots of holidays,' Bernard protested.

'Yeah. In England. I'm talking about you two going abroad. I know Juliet feels the same. Don't you, sis?'

'Yes I do. And if I ever get married, which frankly isn't going to happen. I'll be paying for my own wedding too. The dress is gorgeous, Zoe. But what else did Harrison say?'

'Nothing.' Zoe held the magazine up and showed the image to Rosa and Bernard, who both agreed it was beautiful. 'He invited us to drinks, from seven until nine tomorrow, and asked if you were around. I told him you were at the pub. And off he went. I'm going to go to London after Christmas and see if they've got this in my size. It might even be in the January sales. We should make a day of it, Mum. You, me and Juliet. You can come too, Dad.'

Bernard smiled. 'Thank you, sweetheart. But I think wedding dress shopping is best left to those who understand such things. And what I know about wedding dresses, you could fit on a postage stamp, and still have room to spare.'

'Did he say why he was looking for me?' Juliet persisted.

'Who?' Zoe glanced at her.

'Harrison!'

'No. What colour bridesmaid's dress do you fancy? Pink, I suppose. It's always been your favourite colour. A soft, baby pink might be quite nice. What do you think, Mum?'

'I think it will be lovely, sweetheart. But could we clear the table for lunch, please. Everything's ready, and now that Juliet's home, we can eat.'

'It smells delicious,' Bernard said. 'Are there Yorkshire puddings?'

'I always make Yorkshire puddings with roast beef, darling. Why would today be any different?'

'Or maybe a pale lilac,' Zoe said, moving her magazine from the table and throwing it onto one of the worktops.

'Pour the wine would you, darling?' Rosa said, dishing up the dinner onto the warm plates she had taken from the oven.

'So let me get this straight,' Juliet said, taking off her coat and hanging it up by the door. 'Harrison came here, invited us all to drinks, asked where I was, but didn't say why he wanted to know, and when you told him I was in the pub, he left.'

'Yes, sweetheart,' Rosa said, tossing a piece of beef to Cinnamon, who was sprawled in front of the Aga.

'Why are you still going on about Harrison?' Zoe asked. 'Didn't he see you in the pub?'

'Oh, he saw me. If looks could kill I'd be back at the bottom of the lake. He took one look at me and Dan, turned around, and marched out.'

The room fell silent as her family looked at one another and then at her.

'You and Dan?' Zoe said. 'What were you and Dan doing when he looked at you?'

'Nothing. We were hugging one another and I was telling him how happy I was that he's told his family that he's gay, and in love.'

'Dan's gay?' Bernard said, twisting the lid off a jar of mustard. 'Since when?'

'Since forever,' Juliet said, stepping over Cinnamon and taking a seat.

'I thought he was.' Rosa put the plates on the table and nodded. 'And that explains why he never asked you out.'

'He didn't have to be gay to not ask her out, Mum,' Zoe said. 'He simply might not have fancied her.'

'Yes. But he's always calling her darling and it seems as if he can never keep his hands off her. I always thought it was odd to be so openly and affectionately demonstrative, and yet not to ask her on a date.'

'I see,' said Zoe. 'That makes sense.'

'Perhaps Harrison thought the same,' Bernard said. 'Not wondering why Dan hasn't asked you out, I don't mean. But perhaps he thinks Dan has. Maybe he thinks you and Dan are a couple. Here, sweetheart. Have a glass of wine.'

'Why on earth would he think that?' Juliet asked, taking the glass her dad handed her.

'Oh,' said Zoe. 'That explains a lot. You're right, Dad. That is probably precisely what Harrison thinks. He thinks you're dating Dan. That's why he was cross when he saw you in the pub.'

'Why would Harrison care who I'm dating?'

Again, all three of them looked at her.

'Isn't it obvious, sweetheart?' Rosa said. 'The man is clearly in love with you.'

Juliet's glass slid from her hand, but thankfully it didn't smash. It merely fell on its side and red wine spilt across the table, trickling onto the floor, where Cinnamon eagerly lapped it up.

'Oh God. I'm sorry.' She jumped up, grabbed some kitchen towel and mopped it up from the table. 'But he's not in love with me. He's in love with Kiki.'

Zoe, who had leapt out of the way of the wine-spill, laughed. 'Don't be ridiculous, sis. He's not in love with Kiki. I know she fancies him, but I can assure you it's not reciprocated.'

Bernard wiped some splashes of wine from his Christmas jumper with his handkerchief. 'If anyone's in love with Kiki, I'd say it was old Rufus. Did you see the way he was ogling her last night? And his eyes were following her every move as if they were attached by magnets.'

'Ew,' said Zoe. 'That's creepy.'

'I'm not sure Rufus is capable of love,' Rosa said. 'Although I suppose he must have been once. He did have a son, after all.'

'He didn't have to be in love to have a son,' Zoe said. 'But he was married at the time so let's hope, for his wife's sake, he was.'

'Forget about Rufus.' Juliet sat down again and Bernard refilled her glass. 'The only person I'm interested in is Harrison.'

'We know that, sweetheart.' Bernard put the bottle on the table and patted her hand. 'And as your mother says, Harrison is clearly interested in you.'

'He's not. He can't be. He would've said something if he was. Wouldn't he?'

Zoe sighed. 'You may be my older sister, but you've got a lot to learn about love. Now for heaven's sake, can we eat, please? I've got a pile of bridal magazines to get through, and we've still got all the mince pies to bake, the Christmas cake to ice, presents to wrap, and a whole list of other stuff to do between now and tomorrow night. I've also got to find another dress to wear. I can't wear the same dress I wore to dinner, to the Christmas Eve drinks at The Grange.'

'Oh hell,' said Juliet. 'So have I. But I'm not sure I can afford one.'

'No need to worry about that, sweetheart,' Rosa said, passing around the gravy boat. 'If we don't have to pay for Zoe's wedding, and possibly not for yours, we can dig into our savings and buy you and Zoe something wonderful to wear tomorrow night. I may even buy something lovely for myself.'

Bernard smiled lovingly at his wife. 'Yes, darling. You too shall have a new dress to go to the ball.'

'Oh God. It's not a ball, is it?' Juliet shrieked.

'No, sweetheart. That was merely a figure of speech.'

'Thank heavens for that. Drinks with Harrison, I can probably cope with. Having to dance with him, or worse still, having to watch him spend all night dancing with other people, I definitely couldn't handle.'

'Even now you know he loves you?' Zoe asked, grinning.

'He doesn't love me, Zoe. I don't know why you all think he does, but I can assure you he does not.'

'Let's wait until tomorrow night and see,' Zoe replied.

Without thinking, Juliet glanced up at the kitchen clock. There were only twenty-nine hours, thirty-five minutes and ten seconds until seven o'clock tomorrow night.

Not that she was counting.

Chapter Twenty-Five

Trying to buy an evening dress on Christmas Eve morning in Mistletythe was like being the girl holding the ball on a rugby pitch while surrounded by men who agreed women should be treated as equals. In one shop alone, she had been pushed, elbowed in the back and kicked on the shin, albeit apparently by accident. But she was determined to buy something fabulous, no matter what. Especially now that Harrison was going to so much trouble to make The Grange look festive.

Last night, when she glanced up at The Grange from her bedroom window, she was astonished to see the whole façade was covered in warm, white lights. She could even see, not just one but two, obviously large Christmas trees, also festooned with lights. The man was clearly going to town.

And when she had finally gone to bed, all she could think about were her family's words. They seemed so sure that Harrison was in love with her, or at the very least, interested, and yet none of them had said what made them think so, other than the way he had looked at her. For one moment on Saturday night, even she herself had thought that, when their eyes met after Luke proposed to Zoe. But the way he had behaved afterwards seemed to indicate quite the opposite.

There was also the matter of Kiki. They had clearly had some sort of falling out, but Kiki had told Juliet herself that she and Harrison were dating. Yet Zoe was adamant they weren't. Why would Kiki have lied? And if Harrison truly did have feelings for Juliet, why hadn't he said so? Was it really because he thought she and Dan were an item? Was that what was stopping him?

None of it made any sense. But Zoe was right. Perhaps something would happen on Christmas Eve. Which was why Juliet definitely had to buy a new dress. And not just any dress. It had to be something mind blowing. Luckily, she had taken Dan along.

'I swear,' Juliet said through gritted teeth, 'if one more person elbows me, I'll rugby tackle them to the floor.'

'Oh darling. That I'd like to see. But leave them to me. I'll be your bodyguard.'

That made Juliet laugh. 'I don't want you to be covered in bruises on Boxing Day when Louis arrives.'

'I still can't believe he's coming. I almost died when Dad insisted I put the phone on speaker, and then, after introducing everyone, invited Louis to come and stay. Thank goodness the darling man has to work so will only be coming for the day. I'm really not ready for Noah to try to convert him. I had already explained that to Dad, but you know what he's like.'

'I think it's lovely that they want to meet him, and even nicer that they're happy to welcome him into their home, despite him being an atheist.'

'Don't joke about it, darling. It's terrifying. Meeting your partners' relatives always is. This is it!' He held up a dress from the rack through which he had been browsing, and waved it in front of Juliet. 'The man will be drooling at your feet.'

Juliet laughed again. 'I'm not sure that's the effect I'm going for. I was sort of leaning more towards the, sweep me up in his arms and carry me upstairs to bed, response.'

Dan tutted. 'He'll be doing that too, darling. Trust me. This is the dress. Try it on right now.'

Juliet did as she was told, and when she stepped out of the changing room, not only Dan, but two other men, who were waiting for their respective partners eyed her up and down appreciatively. One of the men was still looking at Juliet when his partner stepped out in the dress she was trying on, and she gave him a hearty slap on the arm.

'Told you, darling,' Dan whispered. 'If that's the effect you can have on two total strangers and one gay man, imagine what you'll do to Harrison. I almost feel sorry for the man. Even though he is such a grump. But you need new shoes. A killer dress demands killer heels. Hurry up and change. We haven't got all day. It's Christmas Eve. Some of the shops will be closing early, and we've got to meet Zoe and your mum. And I've booked you in with my friend, Jerome. You need seriously sexy tresses to complete the picture, and a pedicure and mani, with sparkly nails to match. Oh I'm so excited, darling. Why are you still standing there? Hurry up!'

'I haven't got time to have my hair and nails done, Dan. I promised Mum and Zoe I'd help with the baking this afternoon. We got a lot done yesterday, but there's still a lot to do.'

'Baking? Darling, Juliet. This is your future we're talking about. You can bake for the rest of the holiday. This is Christmas Eve, darling, and it's your time to shine. Now go. We've got things to buy, and places to be. And I've got presents to wrap and put under the tree. Oh my days! All this love stuff has turned me into a poet.'

Chapter Twenty-Six

Harrison walked from room to room, checking that everything was perfect. It had taken some doing, between Sunday morning and this evening, but with Luke, Daphne and Kiki's help, The Grange was ready to receive its guests, and there was still an hour to spare. Plenty of time for him to shower and change. Kiki had gone upstairs at least two hours earlier, and although it had taken more than a small amount of persuasion from him, Daphne had gone to her room just over an hour ago. It always took women far longer than men to get dressed for such occasions. He hoped it would all be worth it.

As he flicked on the final switch for the outside lights, his gaze wandered down towards Mistletoe Row and landed, with little effort, on number 29. From here the cottage looked warm and welcoming and he could just make out the tree, decked with lights, in front of the sitting room window. His gaze wandered upwards to the attic room, which he knew from what Luke had told him, was Juliet's. Was she looking out of her window at The Grange? He could see an amber glow emanating from the room, but the curtains were clearly drawn, and he couldn't see any movement inside.

What would she think when she looked up at the house and saw the lights? Would she be pleased that he had made such an effort to make the house look festive? Or would she be annoyed and feel that he was trying to step into her family's shoes? And although he had personally invited everyone who lived on Mistletoe Row, would any of them turn up? Or would they too feel that the Bows were trying to replace the Bells? He would soon find out.

He ran upstairs to his room, told his voice activated smart speaker to play Christmas music, threw his clothes into the washing hamper and jumped into the shower, singing along with Mariah Carey. He knew exactly what he wanted for Christmas. He simply had no idea how to get it. When they were in the pub on Monday, Kiki had said, much to his annoyance, that money could buy anything. She was wrong. Money couldn't buy love. And love was what he wanted more than anything in the world. If he had to choose tonight, between all his money or love, it would be a no-brainer. Love would win. But not just any love, of course. The only love he wanted; the only love he had ever wanted, was Juliet's. And it made him sick inside to think she may have given that love to someone else. Not that there was anything wrong with Daniel Dobbie, as far as he was aware. Apart from the fact that Juliet appeared to be in love with the man.

And yet something Luke had said had made him think that perhaps he was wrong about Dan and Juliet. When he had told Luke what he had seen on Friday night, of which Luke was apparently unaware, and of what he had seen again in the pub this morning, Luke had shrugged and laughed.

'They've known each other all their lives and they're exactly the same age, bar one month. Of course they're going to be close. But if Juliet has feelings for Dan, she definitely hasn't told Zoe. And Zoe says that she thinks Dan may be gay. I know he looks like a strapping, athletic kind of guy, but he's certainly got a strong feminine side.'

'He calls her darling all the time,' Harrison said. 'He doesn't do that to anyone else. Not that I've heard, at least.'

'But she doesn't call him darling, does she?'

That much was true.

'Every time I see them together they've got their arms around one another,' Harrison moaned.

'But have you actually seen them kiss? Not a kiss on the cheek. I've seen them do that. A real kiss. On the lips.'

He hadn't. But perhaps they didn't like to be overly demonstrative in public.

'There's only one way to find out, bro,' Luke had said. 'Just ask Juliet.'

'That may not be as simple as it sounds.'

'Of course it is. You simply ask her if she's dating Dan, or anyone else? I'd ask her myself, but you've forbidden me from telling her how you feel. Although I suppose I could ask her if she's dating anyone. As her future brother-in-law that shouldn't sound too creepy. I wouldn't want her to think I'm interested for myself. And Zoe would kill me if she thought that. On second thoughts, ask her yourself. And do it tonight. You're not getting any younger, you know.'

'Thanks. I'll bear that in mind.'

And he had been thinking of little else all day.

Chapter Twenty-Seven

Once again Luke came to collect them, but this time Bernard didn't have to ask him to slow down. From the moment he left their front door to the second he arrived at The Grange and pulled up between the two large, brightly lit Christmas trees, he drove at a sensible speed in the icy conditions.

'It's going to snow again tonight,' Bernard said. 'And it's even forecast for tomorrow. I can't recall the last time we had snow on Christmas Day.'

'It was when we lived at The Grange,' Rosa said, snuggled on the back seat beside Juliet, who was seated in the middle between Rosa and Zoe. 'The year before we moved out. I can remember because the boiler broke down on Christmas Eve and we couldn't get anyone out to fix it until the day after Boxing Day. We had to have fires in every room. But at least we didn't have guests that year. We had started to tighten our purse strings.'

She gave a little cough. 'But Luke, the house looks marvellous. You all must have been working very hard.'

Luke laughed. 'Harrison's a slave driver. Only joking. But he certainly knew exactly what he wanted and was determined to get it done in time. What do you think of it, Juliet?'

Her astonishment had increased the closer they had got to the house. 'I think it's spectacular. It reminds me of all the Christmases we spent here. And I know it sounds ridiculous, but the house itself looks happier.'

'That's exactly what Harrison said when we stood outside at dusk. He asked Daphne to turn on all the lights and as the house went from darkness to row upon row of fairy lights, he said it was as if the house had actually smiled, and somehow grown in stature as if it were bursting with pride.' Luke chuckled and threw a quick grin at Juliet as he engaged the handbrake and switched off the engine. 'I told him he must be suffering from exhaustion and was clearly delusional. Either that or he'd started downing a bottle or two of the festive spirit ahead of the rest of us.'

Juliet couldn't help but smile as she got out of the car. She wished she had been standing beside Harrison when he had said that. She would have liked to have seen his face. She glanced towards the door, but this time he didn't come out to greet them.

Another car pulled up beside Luke's and Dan and his entire family piled out. It was a good thing Kevin had an eight-seater.

'Hello darling.' Dan ran over to Juliet and hugged her. Lowering his voice he said, 'I told the family we had to be here at spot on seven. I've got to see the grump's face when he lays his eyes on that dress.'

'I'm feeling really nervous,' Juliet whispered back.

'I'll hold your hand, darling until we get inside.'

He took her hand in his as she waved at Paula, Kevin, Mr and Mrs D, and Noah. She was surprised to see Noah. As the vicar of St Clement's she thought he would be holding an evening service, in addition to preparing for Midnight Mass.

'Who's holding the services this evening, Noah?' Rosa asked, as if reading Juliet's thoughts.

'We had a service between six and seven, but Daniel came and virtually dragged me out at a few minutes to the hour. Having said that, the church was as good as empty. I assume everyone is either on their way, or preparing to come here. I'm expecting everybody at Midnight Mass. And I hope that includes all of you.'

He smiled at Juliet's family, who all nodded enthusiastically.

'There's a first time for everything,' Zoe whispered, beside Juliet. 'You're coming too, Luke.'

'I'll happily go with you. That'll mean I'll actually see you first thing on Christmas morning. What time does it end? Around one a.m.?'

Zoe shrugged. 'No idea. I've never been before. Let's get inside. It's freezing out here.'

Everyone piled inside, but Dan held Juliet back. 'You want to make an entrance, darling. Not go in with the herd. You need him to wonder where you are, and to look for you. And if we go in last, he won't be in a rush to take the coats from anyone behind us.'

'When did you get so good at this?'

He rolled his eyes. 'Years of practice, darling. Right. They've all gone in. If we amble slowly, we should time it perfectly.'

Dan was right. When they walked inside the door, Luke was helping Daphne take coats from everyone in front of them. Harrison must have already taken one armful and hung them up, because when Juliet and Dan stood in front of him, he only had one other coat draped over his arm, as he cheerily wished them Merry Christmas.

In what obviously seemed to Harrison to be an ungentlemanly gesture, if the expression on his face was anything to go by, Dan stepped in front of Juliet and took off his coat, handing it to Harrison with a beaming smile. And then, instead of waiting for Juliet, he walked away and stood beside the sitting room door, turning back to look at them, with his hands shoved in his pockets.

Harrison's frown followed Dan for a moment, and then he turned his attention back to Juliet. Daphne and Luke had left with their arms full of coats, and everyone else had made their way to the sitting room, effectively leaving Harrison and Juliet alone.

Exactly as Dan had shown her, Juliet slowly removed the snood that was covering her hair and neck and was gratified to see Harrison's eyes widen as inch by inch her expertly styled, up do, with delicately curled tendrils hanging at intervals each side, was revealed. He didn't say a word when she gently laid the snood across his forearm, whilst looking directly into his eyes.

A moment later, she turned away from him and slowly and seductively, slid off her coat. The first thing he would see were the gossamer, emerald green and gold strands, dotted with the finest, lightest glitter, like the delicate web of a spider after a morning frost, criss-crossing her naked back.

His eyes would then take in the emerald green velvet of the skirt, which clung to her from her waist to just below her thighs, from where sliver after sliver of alternating, emerald green and gold organza flowed to points, an inch or so below her knees.

Then she would turn, ensuring her coat was held in one hand, away from her body, so that his gaze would fall on the fitted velvet, low-cut bodice, encased in the sheerest emerald green organza covering her décolletage and arms.

As Dan had said when he saw it, the dress revealed nothing, and yet, in a way, everything at the same time.

'And it won't take a genius,' Dan had added, 'to realise that there won't be any underwear beneath that dress.'

From the look on Harrison's face as Juliet handed him her coat, Harrison had figured that much out.

'Merry Christmas, Harrison,' she said, looking deep into his smouldering eyes, and smiling. 'The house looks magical tonight. And there's even a full moon. It's enough to make you believe that anything could happen.' Then she sashayed towards Dan, desperately hoping that she wouldn't topple over in her high-heeled, glittering emerald, evening shoes, because she was absolutely certain that Harrison was watching her every move.

Dan smiled as she reached him, linked her arm through his, and whispered in her ear.

'Bloody hell, darling. That was even better than I expected. The man can't take his eyes off you. This evening should be fun.'

'I need a drink,' Juliet said. 'A large one.'

'Don't forget,' Dan added. 'Throw the man a little smile before we disappear from view.'

She took a deep breath, slowly turning her head until her eyes met Harrison's. A brief smile; the merest lick of her lips, and she turned away again. But not before she saw his jaw drop towards his chest. She could almost hear the gasp escape him.

She wanted to jump for joy. But she didn't want to risk it in her shoes. She would probably break her ankle.

'God. That felt good. Who knew that deep down, I'm nothing but a flirt?'

'You're a goddess, darling. Goddesses don't flirt. They merely mesmerise. Now all we have to do is get rid of Kiki, and find a way to make sure you and Harrison can be alone. But I'm telling you now, if I see that man frown or scowl at you, I'm going to punch him in the face. The season of goodwill, or not.'

Juliet laughed. 'I might do that myself if he tells me to get lost.'

'The man is a grump, darling. Not a complete idiot.'

'Champagne?' Luke appeared from the hall, with Zoe by his side, and a waiter who was carrying a tray of glasses filled virtually to the brim.

'You've got staff?' Juliet was surprised.

'We've got caterers,' Luke said. 'Don't ask me how at such short notice, but it seems that Kiki was right. Money can buy anything.'

Juliet stiffened. 'When did she say that?'

Luke shrugged and glanced at Zoe. 'At the pub on Monday night, I think. Here.' He handed Juliet and Dan a glass. And then his eyes opened wide and he looked Juliet up and down. 'Wow. That's some dress. You and Zoe are determined to outshine everyone tonight.'

Zoe's dress was black, tight-fitting crêpe, with tiny silver hearts embroidered down the gossamer sleeves, but the rest of the dress was plain, and straight, and very sexy. Although according to Dan who helped Zoe choose it, not quite as sexy as Juliet's.

'Thanks,' said Juliet.

'Has Harrison seen it?' There was a look of devilment in Luke's eyes.

'Yes,' she said, with a smile. 'He's seen it.'

A huge grin spread across Luke's face. 'I think tonight is going to be interesting.'

'I hope so,' Juliet replied.

Luke and Dan both burst out laughing and Zoe grinned and winked.

Chapter Twenty-Eight

Harrison wasn't sure what was happening to him. Was he having a heart attack? Or just palpitations? From the moment he had seen Juliet's hair, he had felt the craziest urge to slide his hands into either side, and gently pull her towards him, kissing her glistening, dark cherry lips. And when she had turned her back to him he wanted to get caught in that fabric spiderweb. To say he was knocked for six when she turned around again to face him was an understatement. Had the world spun off its axis? For a moment he was sure it had. She had smiled at him and spoken those words – and the entire universe tilted into an uncontrollable spin. How could one woman make him feel like that?

What was even more distressing, was that he definitely hadn't had the slightest effect on her composure. She was cool, seductive and mind-blowingly sexy, and it didn't even look as if she was trying. And when she tossed him that tiny breadcrumb of a smile as she walked away on that bloody man's arm, he wanted to run after her, get down on his knee, and beg her to marry him right then and there.

But of course, all that would have achieved would have been to make him look like an even bigger fool than he was. She would obviously have said no. She may have even laughed.

He looked down at her coat and snood, shook his head and walked towards the closet, where he hung them up with the others. He was about to go and get a drink, because, boy, did he need one, when the doorbell rang. The only guests he had planned to meet at the door was of course Juliet and her family, so he quickly caught the eye of one of the staff he had employed for the evening, and asked him to 'do the honours'. Then he quickly dashed into the sitting room and grabbed two glasses of champagne.

'Is one of those for me?' Kiki asked, as she sidled up to him.

He shook his head. 'Nope. Sorry Kiki. I need them both.' But he nodded to one of the waiters and the man brought over a tray containing several more.

Harrison emptied one glass and grabbed another as Kiki helped herself.

'Thank you for letting me stay,' she said. 'I can't believe there weren't any flights at all.'

He shrugged. 'Well, it is Christmas. You're welcome to stay as long as you like, Kiki. But I need to ask you something.'

'Yes?' She turned to face him and smiled.

'Did you, by any chance, go to Juliet's room when she was here?'

Kiki shrugged. 'Yes. Just to say hello. I told you I had.'

'Did you?' He frowned. 'I don't remember that. Did you also tell her that you and I were in some sort of relationship?'

'I told her I had been your assistant for several years, and that you and my brother are friends.'

'And that was it?'

She shrugged again. 'I believe so. Why? Has she said anything different?'

'Yes. But I thought she was imagining it. And I can't remember exactly what she said.'

'Well, it's hardly important, is it? This looks like it could be a fun evening.'

He nodded. 'I hope so. Even Grandfather's smiling. And he seems to be standing without using his cane.'

'I noticed that.' She gave Harrison an odd look. 'He's nothing like I expected. I thought he would be some sort of ogre. He's really rather nice.'

'I told you not to believe anything that man said.'

'I know you did. Don't worry, Harrison. I'm a big girl. I can look after myself.'

Harrison smiled. 'I don't doubt that for a second. Excuse me. I think I should be mingling. Have fun.'

'Oh, I intend to.'

Harrison gave her a quick look as he walked away. That almost sounded as though she had something planned. But he wasn't interested in that. He had been scanning the room for Juliet from the moment he entered, and finally he had caught a glimpse of her. She was walking out into the hall. He grabbed another two glasses of champagne from a tray as he passed, leaving his empty glasses in their place, and followed Juliet.

She was walking towards the French windows, leading out onto the terrace at the back of the house. Surely she wasn't thinking of going outside without a coat? It was freezing out there. He needn't have worried. She stopped in front of one set of windows and peered through the glass, as a stream of moonlight bathed her from head to toe.

'It's a beautiful night,' he said, as he drew close.

She spun around, a startled look on her face, her hand on her chest.

'Sorry,' he added. 'I didn't mean to startle you. I seem to be doing that a lot.'

She looked like a frightened doe. Her gaze darted from side to side as if searching for an escape. Was she scared of him?

'Are you okay, Juliet? There's really no need to be frightened. I wouldn't dream of harming a hair of your head.' He stopped in his tracks to prove his point.

She let out a sigh, and shook her head, her tendrils of hair gleaming silver in the moonlight.

'I know you wouldn't. I'm not frightened of you. I ...' She shrugged her shoulders and gave an odd little smile. 'I was embarrassed for being caught.'

'Caught?'

'I was looking at the lake. You can just see a glimpse of it from here. I can still remember how beautiful it looks on a night like this, with the moon trailing across it. It'll be glittering as if it were a pool of diamonds under the snow and ice. I wanted to see it. I'm sorry.'

Harrison let out a breath. 'You don't need to be sorry. And you certainly don't need to be embarrassed. You're welcome to go anywhere you want in this house. To look at anything you want.'

'I don't think your grandad would agree.'

'It's got nothing to do with him.'

She shook her head slowly, but didn't respond.

'If you want to look at the lake,' he added. 'I can get our coats and we can go for a walk.'

She lifted her foot a fraction. 'In these heels? I don't think so.'

'Good point.' A smile crept onto his lips. 'There is another option.'

'Oh?'

'The Lake room has the perfect view.'

She nodded. 'I know. But I thought it was a bit cheeky to wander into one of the bedrooms.'

His smile broadened. His heart picked up a beat or two. 'I'm sure no one will mind. I can go with you. That way you'll have permission.'

She hesitated. Her brows furrowed the merest fraction and she gave him a questioning look.

'Could we? I really would love to see it.'

'Absolutely. So would I. Come on.'

He nodded his head in the direction of the stairs and she hurried to his side. He handed her one of the glasses and she took it with a smile.

'Thank you for this.'

'The champagne?'

She tutted. 'You know that wasn't what I meant.'

He smiled. 'You're very welcome. So, you think the house looks magical?'

He could see the colour flood into her cheeks and her eyelashes flickered for a moment.

'It does.'

'I'm glad you think so. I did it for you.'

She stopped on the stair. 'For me?'

'Because you said the house looked miserable.'

'Oh. Yes. Sorry about that.'

'Don't be sorry. You were right. It did.'

She sipped her champagne and resumed her pace.

'I can't believe you managed to do it all in such a short amount of time. It used to take us weeks.'

'I was lucky. I was able to find the right people at the right time.'

'Yes. I suppose it's true. Money can buy anything. Well almost anything.'

Now it was Harrison who stopped. 'Oh? Is that what you think?'

She looked perplexed. 'Yes. No. I don't know. It was something Luke said tonight. And he was quoting someone else. I do believe money can buy a lot, but it can't buy everything. It can't buy happiness. And it can't buy love.'

'It definitely can't buy love. And you're right. It can't buy happiness either.'

They continued up the stairs in silence for a moment.

Juliet smiled across at him. 'I think we said the other night that we're actually happier in the cottage. But I hadn't realised that until the other day when I came home. I missed this house so much. But mainly, I missed the lake. That sounds silly I know. But it's true.'

'I meant it when I said that you're welcome here. That wasn't just a line.'

'Thank you. That means a lot.'

They walked along the hall towards the room and with his free hand, he opened the door and let her pass, leaving it open behind him.

She looked around the room and gasped.

'Someone's occupying this room.'

He nodded. 'It's mine.'

Now she did look frightened. 'Is this some sort of trick? Do you think this is funny? What were you planning to do?' Her eyes shot to the bed. 'You can't seriously have thought …' Her voice trailed off.

'I hadn't planned anything, Juliet. And no, I didn't think that you would jump into bed with me. I may be an idiot, but I'm not completely mad. I wanted you to see the moon on the lake, and let's be honest, if I had told you this was my room, there was no way you would have come here with me, is there?'

She lowered her eyes and fiddled with her champagne glass. She swallowed deeply and her voice was just above a whisper when she spoke.

'I think we should leave.'

'You haven't looked at the lake.'

She shook her head and took a step towards the door.

'Wait, Juliet,' he pleaded. 'I'll leave. You stay and look at the lake.' He nodded towards the door. 'The key's in the lock. I have no idea why but it is. You can lock the door behind me if you like. I'll see you downstairs later.'

He turned to walk away but as he reached the door she spoke.

'You don't have to go. I'm sorry. I'm behaving like a fool. I know you wouldn't do anything I didn't want you to. I trust you.' She looked surprised as she said that.

'Do you?'

She nodded. 'Yes, Harrison. I do.'

He breathed a sigh of relief and walked towards one of the two windows in the room. 'That's good to know.' He smiled at her and pointed to the other window. 'But just in case you've got any ideas of your own, you look out of that window and I'll look out of this one.'

Her laughter made his heart sing.

'You're safe with me. I promise I'll keep my hands to myself.'

'That's a pity.'

She met his eyes and then quickly looked away, gasping as she looked through the glass, towards the lake.

Harrison did the same and the sight almost took his breath away. He hadn't really looked at the view since he'd been here, but it was stunning. Almost as mesmerising as Juliet. The moon hung low over the trees and cast a higgledy-piggledy silver path through the wood, but when it reached the lake, it fanned out across the entire length, the ice and snow glistening white and silver. Even the bench – their bench – was a gleaming, silver invitation.

He looked at Juliet and watched her face. Her mouth was open just a fraction; her eyes were wide and sparkling in the reflection. Her complexion had an ethereal glow.

He hadn't meant to, but he slowly walked towards her and as he reached her side, she turned her head and met his eyes. He put his glass on the windowsill, slowly raised his hand and slid his fingers into her hair while his other hand circled her waist and then he lowered his face to hers and gently kissed her lips.

She softly moaned his name as he deepened the kiss and pulling her tighter to him, his heart soared as her arms encircled him.

And then, before he knew what was happening, she pushed herself away from him, her hands against his torso, and a look of both disgust and self-loathing on her face.

'This is wrong,' she croaked.

'How can it be wrong, Juliet? I love you.'

She looked astonished. Her mouth fell open and she blinked several times.

'And Kiki? What about her?'

'What's Kiki got to do with anything?'

'Harrison! She's your girlfriend.'

'No she's not. Who told you that? I don't have a girlfriend. Is this just because you're feeling guilty? Because you feel that you may be cheating on Dan?'

'What? How could I be cheating on Dan?'

'You're dating him, aren't you?'

A strange laugh escaped her. 'No. I'm not dating Dan. We're just good friends.'

'Friends with benefits, you mean? Friends who sleep together?'

'Absolutely not. Harrison, you're clearly not aware of this, and I suppose there's no reason why you should be, but Dan is gay. He always has been. Ever since we were young. Although he didn't really understand it at the time. But please don't repeat that to anyone. He's only just told his family and I think he should be the one to tell anyone else.'

Had he heard her correctly? Had she said Dan was gay?

'So you and he really are just good friends? Are you dating anyone?'

She shook her head. 'No. No one.'

He stared at her for a moment or two before he broke into a massive smile. 'Then, unless I'm missing something, if you're not dating anyone, and I'm not dating anyone, why is this so wrong?'

She frowned and looked thoughtful. 'You're definitely not dating anyone?'

'I'm definitely not. But I'd like to. I'd like to very much. Will you go on a date with me, please?'

She shook her head but she was laughing. 'I … I don't what to say. I haven't seen you for twenty years and suddenly you appear and turn my world upside down. I thought I hated you. And then you go and save my life. How am I supposed to feel after that?'

'I apologise. If I'd known saving you would cause you any distress, naturally, I would have let you drown.' He laughed and reached out his hand.

'Please, Juliet. Give me a chance. Give us a chance.'

'Is this really what you want? Do you really want me? I thought … I thought it was all about the house.'

'When?'

'Twenty years ago.'

'It wasn't then. It isn't now. I didn't know grandfather was buying the house. Believe me, if I had, I would have tried to stop him.'

'That would've been even worse. We really needed the money. I only found out the other day, but your grandad actually did us a favour. He had been after the place for a while and on that day, he increased his offer. I was a spoilt sixteen-year-old, who had no idea how the real world worked. To be honest, I'm not sure I've got much of a clue now. But I resented you and blamed you, and myself, for something neither of us did.'

'Are you telling me you were wrong?'

She nodded. 'Completely and utterly. And I am so, so sorry for the dreadful things I said to you that day. The thing was, you made me believe unicorns were real, that Prince Charming existed in the form of you, that my life could be a real-life fairy tale, and then I went home and was told that your grandad had bought our house and we were going to have to move out in a matter of weeks.'

'So you ran to the bus stop and told me exactly what you thought of me.'

'Yes. But I was wrong. You weren't any of the awful things I called you. Part of me hoped you would try to explain. But you only stayed a few weeks, kept yourself to yourself, and then walked out of my life forever.'

'Not forever, Juliet. I'm here now. And I would've been here twenty years ago, but grandfather gave me an ultimatum, and it was one I couldn't ignore. I had to choose between you and Luke's future. And although I've regretted it for most of my life, I chose my brother. I won't go into details now. But one day, I will tell you. As for the things you said, I must admit, some of them cut me to the quick. I've carried those words with me for the last twenty years. I wasn't sure that I could ever forgive you. But when you fell through the ice the other day, I knew I could forgive you anything. And I do. Without reservation.'

She smiled and bit her lower lip. 'So where do we go from here?'

He smiled back and slowly walked towards her. 'That depends on you.'

'On me?'

He nodded. 'I'm waiting for an answer to my question.'

'Your question?'

He nodded again. 'Will you go on a date with me?'

'O-h,' she said, dragging the word out, and smiling seductively. 'Let me think.'

He took her hand in his and gently pulled her to him. 'Time's up. Yes or no?'

She looked up into his eyes and smiled lovingly. 'Well, you did save my life, so I suppose I had better say yes.'

'Yes?' He raised his brows.

She nodded. 'Yes, Harrison. One hundred per cent, yes.'

This time when he kissed her, she didn't push him away. In fact, she took his hand in hers, and, still kissing him, she led him towards his king-sized bed.

Chapter Twenty-Nine

'I hate to say this, Harrison, but we've been in bed for an hour or more. Don't you think we should go back downstairs? We're bound to have been missed.'

'I don't care.' He pulled her naked body closer and kissed her yet again. 'I'll lock the door and we can pretend we're not here if anyone comes looking for us. In fact. I'll send Luke a text and tell him not to.'

'As tempting as that is. And I do mean that. I don't want to get out of your bed, any more than you do. But you did invite all the people tonight. Don't you think it's a bit rude not to put in an appearance?'

'I did. And so did you. I've waited twenty years to be with you. An hour is nowhere near long enough to make up for all that lost time.'

'I agree completely. But your drinks party ends at nine. After that, we can do whatever we like.'

He was kissing her neck but he stopped and looked at her. 'Really? *Whatever* we like? I like a lot of things.' He smiled mischievously.

'So do I. And yes, whatever we like. All night long. Once your guests have gone. Oh. Wait. I've got to go to Midnight Mass. And so have you.'

'Have I?'

'Yes. And I promised Mum and Zoe I'd help with some baking. I should've done it today but I went to town and bought a dress instead.'

'The dress you wore tonight?'

'Yes. The one you threw on the floor.'

'Actually, you threw it on the floor. I just took it off you. But it was well worth going to town for. That is definitely some dress. You know you nearly gave me a heart attack, don't you? I thought that blue dress you wore on Saturday blew my mind, but tonight. I still don't think I've recovered. And I really enjoyed taking it off you.'

'Well, there you are then. If we go back downstairs, you can take it off me again later. And then again after Midnight Mass. And after I've helped Mum, tomorrow, I'll wear a different dress and you can take that off me too.'

'It's Christmas Day tomorrow.'

'I know it is. We can be one another's presents, and slowly unwrap each other.'

'I like the sound of that. Okay. You win. We'll go back downstairs.' He kissed her again. 'In ten more minutes.'

Chapter Thirty

'Where have you been?' Zoe asked Juliet. 'And why is there such a strange smile on your face? Oh my God. You haven't?'

Juliet beamed at her and nodded. 'We have.'

'You and Harrison?'

'No. Me and Rufus.' Juliet laughed and linked her arm through Zoe's. 'Of course me and Harrison. And believe me it was almost worth waiting twenty years for. Apart from the fact that I now realise even more what I've been missing. And I've been missing a lot.'

Zoe burst out laughing too. 'I'm so happy for you, sis. I was beginning to think it would never happen. Luke and I have been trying to think of ways to get you two together since the pair of you came home. We wanted you to be friends, but both of us were certain there was a chance of something more than that. I must tell Luke.'

'Whoa! Perhaps Harrison should be the one to tell him. When we came back downstairs, one of the caterers grabbed him, but he'll be back any second.'

'There he is,' Zoe said.

Juliet looked in the direction of her sister's gaze. Harrison was striding towards them with a breathtaking smile on his face and even from this distance, she could see the passion in his deep brown eyes.

'Now that's a man in love,' Zoe added.

He slipped an arm around Juliet and kissed her on the lips in front of everyone. There were a few gasps, a few claps and several shouts of 'Cheers!'

From somewhere close by, Juliet vaguely heard Dan's unmistakable tones. 'Well done, darling. It's about bloody time.'

Juliet and Harrison laughed into their kiss, and slowly eased away from one another. He gave a little bow to the crowd, held her at arm's length, and, like an actor on stage, presented her by holding out his other hand towards her. She smiled across to him and gave a little curtsy to everyone. And the room burst into raucous laughter and celebrations.

Rosa and Bernard hurried towards her and Harrison, hugging them both in turn.

'Finally,' Rosa said, a wide smile on her face and joyful tears at the corner of her eyes.

'Well,' Bernard said, smiling at Harrison. 'I hope this means you will be staying.'

'I'll be wherever Juliet is,' Harrison replied with a beaming smile.

'Welcome to the family,' said Zoe.

'Welcome to ours,' said Luke. 'It took you two long enough. I was beginning to think we would have to lock the pair of you in a room and throw away the key.'

Harrison gave a devilish smile. 'I was thinking the same thing myself less than fifteen minutes ago.' He winked at Juliet.

Rufus appeared from nowhere. 'So you've finally got the girl. I wish you both happy. But I need a minute of your time, my boy.'

Juliet could feel Harrison tense, but after a moment he smiled at her. 'I'll be back in a second. Don't go anywhere without me.'

'Giving orders already?' Dan said, as he stood at Juliet's side, but he was smiling.

Harrison smiled back. 'Pleading, actually. I don't want to lose her again.'

'I don't think there's much chance of that, do you darling?' Dan kissed Juliet on the cheek.

'Absolutely no chance at all,' she replied, looking into Harrison's smiling eyes, before he turned and walked towards his study, with Rufus at his side.

'Is that carollers I can hear?' Zoe asked.

Luke nodded. 'Harrison thought it might be a good way to bring the evening to a close, but I don't think anyone is ready to leave just yet, and there's plenty of champagne and food.'

The carollers voices grew louder as they came from outside into the hall, and everyone gathered round, joining in with *We Wish You a Merry Christmas*.

'It's such a shame Harrison is missing this,' Juliet told Dan, glancing towards the room where she had watched Harrison and Rufus enter. 'I wonder what Rufus wants to talk about. I really hope it's not me. Harrison told me tonight that twenty years ago, Rufus made Harrison choose between me and Luke.'

Dan gasped. 'The bastard!'

Juliet shook her head. 'Please don't say anything about it to anyone, especially not Luke, because I don't know the details and I don't want to cause any problems.'

'Especially as you're all so happy now. My lips are sealed, darling. So tell me, what was Harrison like? I assume he wasn't scowling when you finally surrendered to his wild passions.'

Juliet laughed. 'You've been reading too many romance novels. But actually, it was him who surrendered to mine. Although how do you know we did anything?'

'Darling, please. Even if you had a beacon flashing on the top of your head saying, 'Just had incredible sex,' it couldn't *be* more obvious. I can see it on your face. And I saw it on his. And that man is definitely head over heels in love. So Merry

Christmas, darling. You've got the icing on the cake. I'll grab us more champagne.'

'It seems you won.'

Juliet turned to find Kiki standing behind her.

'Won? I wasn't aware it was a competition. Tell me, Kiki. Why did you lie about you and Harrison?'

Kiki sipped her champagne and shrugged. 'Only a fool would let that man go without a fight. But you got him. So congratulations. I'm moving on to greener pastures.'

'Really?'

Kiki nodded and raised her glass in the air as Dan returned with drinks. 'Merry Christmas.'

'And to you.'

Kiki walked away without so much as a smile.

'I really don't like that bitch,' Dan said, handing Juliet a glass of champagne. 'Oh look. Harrison's coming back. I'll leave you to him, darling. See you later. But don't do anything I wouldn't do.'

'Is there anything you wouldn't do?' Juliet asked, with a laugh.

'No, darling. Not a single thing.' Dan waved as he walked away.

'That didn't take long. Is everything okay? He hasn't given you another ultimatum, has he?'

Harrison pulled her into his arms and kissed her in response, and when he released her he was smiling oddly.

'No. And if he had I would've told him where to shove it. It seems he's going away on Boxing Day. Possibly for some time.'

'Going away? Where? Because of us?'

Harrison shook his head. 'He hasn't decided where, but to somewhere hot. He's had enough of the cold and snow, and the warm weather will be better for his joints.' He gave a little laugh. 'Apparently, he isn't going alone.'

'Oh. Who's going with him?'

Harrison raised his brows and smiled. 'Guess.'

Juliet furrowed her brows for a split second. 'Oh my God! Not Kiki?'

Harrison nodded. 'It seems they've become quite fond of one another in the last couple of days.'

Juliet couldn't believe it. 'She just told me she was moving on to greener pastures.'

'Did she indeed? I hope she won't be too disappointed.'

'What will you do without her? Wasn't she your executive assistant?'

'Yes. It seems I have a vacancy to fill.' He pulled her closer. 'May I ask you something?'

'Anything. Oh. Are you going to ask me to become your executive assistant?'

He shook his head. 'No. I've got an entirely different position for you in mind.'

'Oh really? I do need a job.'

'We can discuss that later. This isn't about work. If I asked you to move away from here, from this house, would you do it?'

'Of course I would.'

'Even if it meant never setting foot here again?'

'Yes. But I'd have to come home to see my family.'

He let out a sigh. 'I knew I didn't need to ask. I'm sorry I did. But that old man still found a way to get to me. He said I'd better make sure it was me you wanted and not the house.'

'Harrison!' She pulled away from him, more than a little hurt. 'How could you think that for a second?'

'I don't. I didn't. But you don't know how that man gets under my skin. I'm sorry, Juliet. I had to be sure. Forgive me.'

She sighed and stepped back into his arms, as the carollers burst into *Silent Night*.

'I do forgive you. I suppose, in a way, I can't blame you for asking. I have been rather obsessed with the place. But if I had to choose between you and the house, there really is no contest. I'd choose you, Harrison. Without hesitation.'

She kissed him passionately while the carollers finished *Silent Night* and got to the end of *God Rest Ye Merry Gentlemen.*

'This is going to be the best Christmas ever,' he said, when they finally parted lips.

Juliet had a sudden thought. 'If things work out between Kiki and your grandad, do you think she'll be moving into here?'

'No. Apart from the fact that Kiki prefers bright lights and lots of parties, it's not his house.'

'It's not? Oh, you mean you'll inherit it when he dies?'

'No, my darling Juliet. I mean it's not his house. It's mine. And don't get cross because I didn't have any idea until I was thirty, but it's been mine all along. The old man bought it with my money. Well, with the money Dad left and funds from an ancient trust. Grandfather made me believe it was his money and that he was taking care of me and Luke out of the goodness of his heart, rather than the fact that he was the trustee of Dad's estate.'

'Oh Good grief. That's dreadful.'

He raised his brows. 'That I own the house?'

'No. What Rufus did.'

Harrison shrugged. 'He is who he is. He'll never change. Thankfully, Dad was nothing like him, and Mum was the epitome of sweetness and light. I think I take after them. At least I hope to God I do.'

'You do, Harrison. You're nothing like Rufus. I wish I could've met them.'

'So do I. They would've loved you almost as much as I do.' He glanced around the room. 'Are these people ever going to leave? I want to go back upstairs and admire the view.'

She grinned up at him. 'I think everyone's going to be staying on for a while yet.' She grabbed his hand. 'There's a pretty good view from the Rose room too. Allow me to show you. And that door also has the key in the lock. I noticed that the night I stayed here.'

Chapter Thirty-One

Juliet rolled over and reached out her arm for Harrison. He wasn't there. She sat upright and glanced around the room. He was nowhere to be seen. She looked at her watch. Eight-thirty on Christmas morning. Where could he have gone?

Last night, after they had spent an hour or so in her old bedroom, they'd returned downstairs to find the party was finally coming to an end. They chatted with the guests remaining until it was time for Midnight Mass. Taking several cars, and Juliet going with Harrison, they went to St Clement's and when they came out, it was snowing.

'Are you spending the night at The Grange?' Rosa asked her.

'If you don't mind, Mum. I promise I'll come home first thing in the morning and help prepare Christmas dinner.'

'Oh sweetheart, don't worry about it. Your father and I can manage perfectly well. Zoe's also going to be at The Grange tonight, so come home when you like, but it would be nice to have dinner together.'

I'll definitely come home in plenty of time for that,' Juliet had promised.

She had spent the most glorious night in Harrison arms. And in his bed. But now, he was nowhere to be seen.

'Morning. Merry Christmas!' He appeared in the doorway with a breakfast tray laden with smoked salmon, caviar and scrambled eggs, two glasses of orange juice and a bottle of champagne.'

'Merry Christmas,' she said, beaming at him. 'For a dreadful moment I thought I'd imagined last night when I woke up alone, but I saw I was in your room so I knew some of it had happened.'

He looked contrite for a second before he smiled. 'I'm sorry. I should've waited until you woke up. But I was excited to start the day.' He placed the tray on the bedside table, and bent down to kiss her. 'Last night was the best night of my life. I love you, Juliet.'

'Best night so far,' she said. 'I love you too. I promised Mum I'd go home this morning. You're welcome to join me, but I assume you'll be having Christmas dinner here.'

He nodded. 'I suppose I should. Especially as Grandfather is planning on leaving tomorrow. Who knows when, or if, he'll come back. I may actually pay him to stay away. Although he is family, so we'll see. We could always have dinner at both. We're having ours this evening. You're having yours around two, I think you said.'

Juliet nodded. 'Two Christmas dinners? I'm not sure I could manage two.'

He grinned. 'We can work some of it off, in between. What do you say? Even if we don't eat much at either, it'll be fun to spend out first Christmas together with both families, don't you think? And we've got plenty of food here if your mum doesn't have enough.'

Juliet was excited at the prospect. 'I'll text Zoe now and see what she thinks, and I'll call mum after that. Are you sure, Harrison?'

'It means I get to spend all day with you. Of course I'm sure.'

Juliet sent her a text and got a reply a few minutes later while she and Harrison were eating breakfast. Zoe had said yes, and then Juliet called her mum who loved the idea.

'We're all set,' Juliet said. 'But it means I need to go and help prepare all the extra veg.'

'I can come and help with that.' Harrison removed the empty plates and poured each of them another glass of champagne which he placed on the bedside table. 'But first I need to play with my favourite present for a while.'

He pulled the duvet over them and Juliet burst into laughter.

Chapter Thirty-Two

Christmas Day was beyond Juliet's wildest dreams. They spent the morning at the cottage, with Harrison, Luke and her dad peeling vegetables, while she, Zoe and Rosa made mince pies, sausage rolls and cinnamon biscuits which Juliet and Zoe iced with hearts and everyone's names. Cinnamon, the dog, was all over Harrison like a rash, and not sprawled in front of the Aga for once.

'I think you've got Cinnamon's seal of approval', Juliet said.

Harrison laughed. 'That's good to know. I just wish the approval wasn't quite so furry, or so slobbery.'

Rufus and Kiki had chosen to stay at The Grange. They had been invited, but everyone was glad of their decision. And everyone speculated whether their 'relationship', whatever it was, would last.

They opened presents, and Harrison was delighted with the present Juliet gave him. It was a bronze figurine of a knight in armour on a white-glazed horse.

'Well, you did save my life, so you were my knight in shining armour when I bought it. Now that's even more the case.'

'I love it, Juliet. It'll take pride of place on my desk. I've got you something, but I'm not saying what. You'll have to wait and see.'

'You've got me a present? What is it?' Juliet shrieked.

'Patience,' Harrison replied.

They drank champagne with their lunch and brandy with their Christmas pudding and then after playing games and drinking coffee, Harrison said he had to go but would be back in a moment.

'But aren't we all going to The Grange soon?' Juliet asked.

'We are. But there's something I need to do first. Don't go anywhere.' He kissed her and smiled. 'Luke. I need to borrow you for a while.'

'Don't be long,' Zoe said, kissing Luke as if she wouldn't be seeing him for hours.

Cinnamon got up from in front of the sitting room fire and raced after Harrison, barking.

'Cinnamon's missing you already,' Juliet said. 'And she's not the only one.'

'Really girls,' said Bernard. 'They'll only be gone five minutes.'

'You've forgotten what it's like to be young and in love,' Rosa said.

Bernard smiled lovingly. 'I may have forgotten what it's like to be young, darling, but I know what it's like to be in love. I've been in love with you since the day we met.'

Rosa blew him a kiss and smiled. 'And the same goes for me, my love.'

Cinnamon came back, plonked herself in front of the fire and let out a resounding and rather smelly, fart.

Chapter Thirty-Three

Juliet opened the cottage door half an hour or so later, and couldn't believe her eyes. Nor could the rest of her family if their shouts of delight were anything to go by.

Two of the vintage, open top carriages that had been sold with the house were sitting on Mistletoe Row. Each had white and silver ribbon tied all the way around them, but the one in front, had pink roses pinned to the ribbons, and pink rose petals strewn inside. Luckily, there was no breeze today and the predicted snow, had not arrived, so far.

The second carriage had two superb grey horses pulling it, but it was the first carriage that took Juliet's breath away. It was pulled by two magnificent white horses but when she looked at them she saw that they had white, sparkly pointed cones tied with ribbon, around their foreheads and lengths of iridescent streamers falling gently from their manes.

Several people on Mistletoe Row had come to their doors to see what was going on, and customers flocked out from The Mistletoe pub, including Dan and his family.

Oh Harrison! They're wonderful.' Juliet couldn't believe what he had done.

'They may not be unicorns, exactly,' Harrison said. 'But they're trying very hard to be. And I may not be Prince Charming, but I'll spend the rest of my life getting as close to that as I can.' He bent down on one knee in the snow and opened the lid of a tiny, antique box. 'This was my mother's engagement ring. I'll buy you another of your own if you say yes, but in the meantime, will you marry me, Juliet Bell? Will you make me the proudest, happiest man in the world and say you'll be my wife? I know we've only, technically, been on a couple of dates. One twenty years ago and one last night, if that counts as a date. But I've loved you for twenty years and I'll love you till the day I die. And if you think that it's too soon, I'll ask you every day until you finally say yes.'

Juliet's mouth fell open and she stared at him for a second. 'Oh God, Harrison. Of course I'll be your wife. I'll be anything you want as long as I can spend the rest of my life with you.'

'Really?' He beamed at her, got to his feet and slid the ring on her finger.

It fitted perfectly and the magnificent, entwined diamonds sparkled as she marvelled at their beauty.

'Because I do need a new executive assistant, as it happens,' Harrison added.

Juliet burst out laughing. 'Are you offering me the job?'

He shook his head. 'No. But I do want you to be my partner, not just in our personal lives, but in my business, too.'

'Oh for God's sake, man. Just kiss her, will you?' It was Dan's voice and he was out of breath. He'd clearly run from the pub to get a better view.

Harrison looked at Dan and smiled.

'Thanks. I'll do that.' His eyes were filled with love as he smiled at Juliet and pulled her into his arms. 'I love you, Juliet. You are my heart and soul. My Lady of the Lake.'

'And you have made unicorns real. You're my Prince Charming. I love you, Harrison Bow. And this ring is perfect. I don't want another. I absolutely love it.'

Juliet and Harrison smiled adoringly at each other, and kissed, as everyone, especially Rosa, Bernard, Zoe and Luke clapped and cheered. Even Cinnamon's bark sounded congratulatory.

As if on cue, soft flakes of snow fell gently from the sky, the bells of St Clement's started ringing, and via the open door of the cottage next to number 29, carollers on the radio boomed out, *Joy to the World.*

'Oh my days,' Dan said, in the campest voice ever. 'You couldn't make this stuff up. Even the heavens approve, darling. Congratulations and Merry Christmas one and all.'

Juliet was far too busy kissing Harrison to reply.

MERRY CHRISTMAS!

Coming soon

Return to Lily Pond Lane

A new book in the Lily Pond Lane series

A Note from Emily

Thank you for reading this book. A little piece of my heart goes into all of my books and when I send them on their way, I really hope they bring a smile to someone's face. If this book made you smile, or gave you a few pleasant hours of relaxation, I'd love it if you would tell your friends.

I'd be really happy if you have a minute or two to post a review. Just a line will do, and a kind review makes such a difference to my day – to any author's day. Huge thanks to those of you who do so, and for your lovely comments and support on social media. Thank you.

A writer's life can be lonely at times. Sharing a virtual cup of coffee or a glass of wine, or exchanging a few friendly words on Facebook, Twitter or Instagram is so much fun.

You might like to join my Readers' Club by signing up for my newsletter. It's absolutely free, your email address is safe and won't be shared and I won't bombard you, I promise. You can enter competitions and enjoy some giveaways. In addition to that, there's my author page on Facebook and there's also a new Facebook group. You can chat with me and with other fans and get access to my book news, snippets from my daily life, early extracts from my books and lots more besides. Details are on the 'For You' page of my website. You'll find all my contact links in the Contact section following this.

I'm working on my next book right now. Let's see where my characters take us this time. Hope to chat with you soon.

To see details of my other books, please go to the books page on my website, or scan the QR code below to see all my books on Amazon.

Contact

If you want to be the first to hear Emily's news, find out about book releases, enter competitions and gain automatic entry into her Readers' Club, go to: https://www.emilyharvale.com and subscribe to her newsletter via the 'Sign me up' box. If you love Emily's books and want to chat with her and other fans, ask to join the exclusive Emily Harvale's Readers' Club Facebook group.

Or come and say 'Hello' on Facebook, Twitter and Instagram.

Contact Emily via social media:
www.twitter.com/emilyharvale
www.facebook.com/emilyharvalewriter
www.facebook.com/emilyharvale
www.instagram.com/emilyharvale

Or by email via the website:
www.emilyharvale.com

Printed in Great Britain
by Amazon